Colton Destiny

JUSTINE DAVIS

First published in Great Britain 2013
by Mills & Boon, an imprint of Harlequin (UK) Limited.
Large Print edition 2013
Harlequin (UK) Limited,
Eton House, 18-24 Paradise Road,
Richmond, Surrey TW9 1SR

© Harlequin Books S.A. 2012

ISBN: 978 0 263 23781 8

Special thanks and acknowledgment to Justine Davis for her contribution to The Coltons of Eden Falls miniseries.

Harlequin (UK) policy is to use papers that are natural, renewable and recyclable products and made from wood grown in sustainable forests. The logging and manufacturing process conform to the legal environmental regulations of the country of origin.

Printed and bound in Great Britain
by CPI Antony Rowe, Chippenham, Wiltshire

"I thought of leaving, once."

Emma gave him a startled look. "Leaving... Paradise Ridge? Or your faith?"

"Both."

Caleb stopped, stunned that he had said it, that he had told this stranger, this woman, this English, what he had told no one else. Ever.

"I've found," Emma said, "that it's never a good or successful idea to run away from something."

"What did you mean, when you said I didn't have to worry?"

"I've turned up a couple of possible leads. They stopped an older man driving a van with a couple of young girls in it."

Caleb drew back sharply. "Hannah?"

"No, sorry," Emma said quickly. "Neither girl is a match to any of ours."

Any of ours.

She'd said it as if she truly felt it. As if the missing girls were a part of her own community.

Lovely, empathetic and smart—she was all of that.

And to him, apparently, dangerous.

Dear Reader,

One of the most popular stories in fiction is the "fish out of water." It's basically a tale of someone cast into a world strange to them, where they don't have the skills to survive, or don't have the knowledge of the culture to keep from drawing unwanted and sometimes painful attention to themselves, a world where they quite simply Don't Belong.

This would be me and, say, computer programming. Call me clueless, but I have no idea. I'm just glad others do. Some days I wonder what life would be like without technology, what it would be like to simply unplug.

The Amish have chosen to live that life free of those electronic ties. Their world is above all peaceful, and also separate, yet it seems inevitable that now and then our world will intrude into theirs. Such is the case in this story, where the clash of worlds is cold and harsh, yet out of the collision grows an unexpected connection between two people with the odds stacked against them. Can the "fish out of water" make the changes necessary to get to her happy ending?

I hope you enjoy it.

Justine Davis

JUSTINE DAVIS

Justine Davis lives on Puget Sound in Washington State, watching big ships and the occasional submarine go by, and sharing the neighborhood with assorted wildlife, including a pair of bald eagles, deer, a bear or two and a tailless raccoon. In the few hours when she's not planning, plotting or writing her next book, her favorite things are photography, knitting her way through a huge yarn stash and driving her restored 1967 Corvette roadster—top down, of course.

Connect with Justine at her website, justinedavis.com, at Twitter.com/Justine_D_Davis, or on Facebook at Facebook.com/JustineDareDavis

Chapter 1

"Hey, tomato-head."

For an instant Emma Colton thought she'd somehow slipped back in time, that she was back on the ranch being rudely awakened by her annoying brother Tate, who was three years older and had teased her incessantly about her rather bright red hair.

Clutching her phone, she blinked the sleep out of her eyes, the sight of the familiar bedroom of her Cleveland apartment orienting her back into the present. Still, as she shoved her tangled hair away from her face, she felt a tiny frisson of relief that it was still the darker, richer auburn of adulthood. That made her smile, until she realized what time it was.

She yawned. "You don't even have the excuse of a different time zone, bro. This better be good."

"I take back *tomato-head. Sleepyhead* fits better," Tate Colton said.

"It's five in the morning. I thought I was the workaholic in the family."

"Please. It comes with the Colton name. You're just worst than most. Except maybe Uncle Joe."

She laughed, humor restored. The man they'd grown up calling Uncle Joe, although he was in fact their late father's cousin, was indeed dedicated to his work. That hadn't prevented him from standing in for their deceased parents on occasion. Like every Colton, he took family responsibilities very seriously.

Almost as seriously as he took his job as president of the United States.

"So what is it that has you waking me up at this hour?"

"I need your help, little sister."

Something had changed in her brother's deep voice. The teasing note had vanished, replaced by a grim seriousness. Instantly she responded, sitting up straight, shoving aside the warmth of the covers.

"What?"

"I've got three missing girls."

As a Philadelphia police detective, Tate having a case of even three missing girls sadly wasn't shocking. Nor would that alone necessitate this early-morning call to her; if he needed FBI help on a case, he had his own contacts. Not that the name Colton wasn't enough to get him in about any door he wanted at the Hoover Building.

"Why me?" she asked. "Not that I don't mind giving you wise advice, even though you never take it, but—"

"They're Amish."

Emma went very still. "Three?"

"Yes."

"When?"

"Two weeks. The usual reluctance to involve outsiders."

She knew it too well. "How old?"

"Sixteen to nineteen."

"Rumspringa?" Emma asked. Growing up on the family ranch in Eden Falls, Pennsylvania, the Amish and their ways had always been part of the fabric of her life. *Rumspringa,* that time when young people are allowed to explore the outside world, then make their own decision on whether to return to the religion and simple lifestyle of the Amish, had always fascinated her as a teenager. She simply couldn't picture why anyone would voluntarily leave behind the world of convenience and technology for such…deprivation. Yet eighty percent of them did.

Now she wasn't quite so arrogant about her assumptions. She'd seen enough in her years as an FBI agent to understand the appeal of pulling back from the hectic, crazy—and sometimes perverted—world of today.

She realized she was tracing the intricate pattern of the quilt on her bed. An exquisitely designed and handmade Amish quilt, a traditional diamond-on-point pattern in soothing blues, that she'd brought with her from home. Her mother had purchased it from one of their neighbors, had loved it and cared for it so well it seemed almost new. It had come to her as the eldest daughter, after that horrible, shocking day in September 2001, the day that had stolen the loving, generous couple who had taken them all in, adopted them and given them a life beyond anything they ever could have hoped for—

"Emma?"

She snapped out of her reverie. "Sorry. What?"

"I said yes, *Rumspringa.* They're all from Paradise Ridge."

That brought it even closer to home for her; Paradise Ridge literally bordered the Colton ranch. She might even know the families, she thought with a sudden qualm. They had often bought fresh produce and milk from the local farmers.

She had a sudden vivid flash of memory. A young Amish girl near her own age of ten, from when she and her father, Donovan Colton, had stopped to offer assistance to a driver of one of the iconic Amish carriages that added tourist-drawing quaintness to the Pennsylvania countryside. One of those tourists had passed too close in their rental car, clipping the corner of the carriage and sending the right rear wheel onto rain-softened ground, and then proceeded merrily on their way, either uncaring or oblivious to damage done.

She remembered her father pulling the ranch truck up behind the carriage, angling it so that no oncoming car could repeat the incident.

The first concern of her father, a horseman of many years, was the welfare of the animal pulling the carriage. Emma herself had been fascinated by the child who remained in the carriage while her father had gotten out to inspect the damage. She remembered the girl's simple dress, in contrast to her own jeans and T-shirt. She remembered the vivid blue of her eyes as she peeked out to stare in apparent equal fascination at Emma. The only thing she remembered from the conversation between the adults was the Amish man's quiet acceptance; he expected

no better from the English, as they called anyone not Amish.

She shook her head, ordering herself to stop
meandering and pay attention.

"You think your case is connected to mine."
It wasn't a question. Didn't really have to be.
But Tate echoed her own thoughts on the mat-
ter anyway.

"I think the likelihood of two independent serial kidnappers—and maybe killers—targeting
the exact same class of victims, even three hundred miles apart, is slim."

"But possible."

"Anything's possible. But likely?"

"No."

Sometimes both their jobs relied on simply
going with the odds, Emma thought. Still she
hesitated. She was reluctant to abandon, even
temporarily, her own case. She had not just
three, but a string of missing girls going back
nearly three months. But because of that reluctance to involve outsiders, and even more to involve federal outsiders, she'd been called in so

late there had been little to find, and the suspect's trail and the case had quickly gone cold.

Because they'd relocated to Pennsylvania?

"I need you, Emma. You've been working your case long enough, you'll catch anything that might prove or disprove that mine are connected. And you always did relate better to them than any of us."

Not that any of the Colton brood didn't get along, Emma thought. They'd been taught to respect their quiet, peaceful neighbors and appreciate their industrious ways. But Tate was a Philadelphia cop and had come a long way from those youthful, halcyon days on the ranch.

"All right," she said decisively. "I'll be on my way."

"Text me your flight number. I'll pick you up, bring you up to speed on the way to the ranch."

Emma hung up and scrambled out of bed. She called her supervisory agent and left a long voice mail explaining, emphasizing the likely connection to their case to head off any dissent about her being called in by her brother. It was legit, she told herself. If the cases were related, then it crossed state borders and they were involved anyway.

Then she made a reservation for the next flight from Cleveland to Philadelphia. She could probably drive it in about the same amount of time, but wanted to arrive fresh and have a chance to study the pictures and basic details Tate was sending.

Her timeline now set, she showered, quickly dried her hair and pulled it into her usual ponytail. Then she went about the business of packing, although since she and her family had enough clothing left permanently at the ranch to handle everything but the longest visit, it was mainly toiletries and the rather severe pantsuits she generally wore. They were expensive, yes, but subtly so and made to last.

She'd long ago decided she wasn't going to stress out over what to wear to present the proper image; she'd found a style that worked, plain, simple, yet exquisitely cut to flatter, and bought several in the colors she considered acceptable for work—black, dark blue or gray. Not only was it easier, but if she was always wearing the same thing, her attire—and the severe hairstyle—never distracted from her professional demeanor. Sometimes she even resorted to dark-framed glasses to somewhat mask the vivid green of her eyes.

Overall, she strove for a neutral, businesslike look. It was helpful not only with civilians, but with her male colleagues, as well. She had enough trouble with assumptions people made about her, from riding on the Colton name to being a "poor little rich girl," and she didn't want to add to them with any blatantly upscale clothing, fancy jewelry or anything else that might remind people of her background. Especially her connection to Joseph Colton, who was, in essence, the boss of all her bosses.

She shook off the old concerns, went to the nightstand and took out her weapon. With no children in the apartment, she kept the Glock 23 ready for use, and she slipped it into the holster at her waist. It had become a part of her now, and she was, sometimes to her brother's dismay, a better shot than he was. Their phone calls to compare proficiency scores had become a tradition.

Emma smiled. She was so lucky. Tate was the best of big brothers, even if he was a bit overprotective. And as for her big brother Derek... Well, Derek was their rock, his steadfast, solid goodness something they had all clung to at one time or another. And when their parents had left the ranch to him in their will, a will executed far too early, after the vicious sneak attack on September 11, 2001, every shaken Colton child had felt a tiny bit safer knowing Derek would see to it that the ranch remained the refuge it had always been for all of them.

Gunnar, on the other hand...

She couldn't worry about her troubled, antisocial oldest brother just now. She'd see him soon enough, although she didn't expect much change.

Despite the grimness of the reason for the trip, she was looking forward to it. She hadn't been home in a while and hadn't expected to make it before the holidays.

She smiled at the thought of seeing the kids, as she always thought of her sister, Piper, and little brother, Sawyer. She wondered if they were still squabbling, eleven-year-old Sawyer, with his knack for sarcasm, constantly teasing his big sister, and Piper responding with typical six-teen-year-old drama. The girl was tall, five foot nine and still growing, and Emma suspected Sawyer's fear that she might end up taller than he, even when he was grown up, was behind a lot of his jabs at the sister he called an Amazon.

As she headed to the airport, she felt the usual pang that accompanied thoughts of her young-est sibling. Sawyer had been an infant when he'd come to them, practically a newborn. He'd never had the chance to know the kind, generous, dy-namic couple that had adopted him. For a long time they were afraid they were going to lose him back into the system because of the death of Donovan and Charlotte Colton. Derek, ever the rock even at twenty-two, had spearheaded the Colton resistance to the very idea of losing the baby who was the last piece of their parents' grand plan. A contingent had flown in from the Texas Coltons to stand with them, impressive enough, but a brief yet powerful video statement made by then-senator Joseph Colton had put the cap on the affair. As a result, baby Sawyer had gone home with his adoptive family.

She realized suddenly why her mind had veered onto this track. The possible loss of their baby brother had been yet another horrific blow to a family that had already lost so much. The Amish community was like one huge family, and they'd been struck again and again. And no family court hearing could restore their children to them.

It was up to her, and now her brother, to find them and bring them home.

"Thanks, sis," Tate said again. "Any hassle?"

Emma glanced at her brother. He drove as he did anything physical, with an understated ease. He was six foot one, which meant she had to look up at him, even sitting in the passenger seat of his unmarked city car. He glanced at her when she didn't immediately answer. His eyes were as gorgeous as ever, that almost turquoise-blue that had sent her female schoolmates into raptures, embarrassingly, when he'd stumble across them giggling in the kitchen of the big ranch house at the Double C.

"No," she answered. "Not a bit." She paused. Her brother, knowing her well, waited. "Of course, I left the message on his office voice mail. He would have gotten it while I was in the air."

"So he couldn't call and yell until he'd had time to calm down?" Tate grinned at her, then turned his eyes back to the busy street leaving the airport. "You always did know how to get your way."

"You're just saying that because you never figured out how to be subtle."

"You mean devious?" Emma grinned back at him, not offended in the least, before he added,

"But at least I learned it's easier to beg forgiveness than ask permission."

They laughed with the ease of siblings who had grown into a comfortable, loving adult relationship, who looked back on their childhood with fondness. Their lives had been blessed, and even the horrible loss they'd suffered on September 11 couldn't change that.

"Do you still think about them a lot?" Emma knew she didn't have to explain.

"Every day," Tate said quietly. "They saved us all, gave us a life we never, ever would have had."

"And they gave us each other," Emma said. "Brothers and sisters we never would have had."

"Yes." Tate glanced at her. "They saw to it we would never be alone again."

Emma sighed. It had taken them a very long time to reach this point. Charlotte—for whom the ranch had been named—and Donovan Colton had been forces of nature, and Emma didn't think any of them ever got past thinking of them as larger-than-life.

"At least they saw Butterfly Wings come to life."

"That's right," Tate agreed. "They got to see that dream come true."

The nonprofit organization dedicated to helping inner-city kids was flourishing, and each adult Colton put in their time to make sure it stayed that way. Each one of them knew too well they could have ended up in worse shape than some of these kids if not for the generous, loving couple who had adopted them all.

The thought of kids at risk jolted her back to the reason she was here in the first place. It was time to quit dwelling on her own happy childhood and concentrate on trying to get these innocent girls back to finish theirs.

Chapter 2

Emma had noticed the folders wedged next to the driver's seat and reached for them.

"These are the full files?"

Tate nodded as he negotiated the transition to Interstate 95 leaving the airport. Emma began to read. Tate had emailed her the basics, but to her dismay there wasn't much more here. The details on each case were sketchy; either no one had seen much or they weren't talking.

Or the kidnappers were very, very thorough.

She felt the old chill start to creep up her spine. She fought it down. She knew the old memories colored her reactions, but she refused to let them affect her professional conduct. She'd passed her psych, been declared fit for duty, and she was going to see it stayed that way.

"You okay?"

Damn, did the man never miss a thing? Of course, he was probably haunted by his own memories of past cases, which perhaps made him a bit more sensitive than a non-cop would be. For a guy, Tate was pretty sensitive to begin with. For a brother, he had moments that stunned her.

"I'm fine. Perverted men who target women just make me angry."

"I know. That's why I wanted you here. You've got the fire for it like no one else. And you've got an understanding of the people no one else I know has."

Emma gave her brother a sideways look. They rarely spoke of her nightmare ordeal anymore within the family—not directly anyway. And she preferred it that way. Those nine horrific days were history, and that's where they were going to stay. She'd be damned if she'd let that piece of scum she refused to identify by name even in her mind have any effect on her at all.

She'd worked hard for two years to get past what had happened to her. And had almost lost it all when some crazy judge who cared more for the rights of the criminal than the rights of the victims had found a piece of evidence logged in on the wrong place on a form and used it as justification to grant an appeal. So now she was looking at going through it all again, all the testifying, the nightmare of remembering.

But she would do it. She wasn't a Colton for nothing, and she would put that monster away again. And again and again if she had to.

"Not to mention," Tate added drily, "you know the countryside like the back of your hand."

"Hey, hey," she responded with an automatic protest born out of all the times Tate had been the one sent out to retrieve her from wherever she'd wandered. "It's not my fault you were always hungry so you were the one in the house pestering Mom before dinner was ready."

"I just never understood the fascination," Tate said.

That much was true, she knew. She'd always had a fascination with the land itself that her siblings didn't have. They did, however, appreciate the ranch and the life it gave them. As a child she'd spent hours studying plants and trees, wondering how they grew, how it was they reached for the sun, how, without a brain, they even knew where the sun was. She'd planned on continuing that study in her schooling, thinking a plant biologist might just be the coolest job ever.

And then, in her first year of college, everything changed. Those crazed men had destroyed so much more than buildings that day. And once she realized they didn't care, and that there were countless others lined up, hoping for a chance to do more of the same, willing to die simply to murder those who didn't follow their God, her path had become clear. She'd changed her major, determined then and there she would become part of the line that would stop such horror from ever occurring again on American soil.

She wasn't sure she was accomplishing that from the field office in Cleveland, although it had on occasion whimsically occurred to her that with their feelings about music, the Rock and Roll Hall of Fame and Museum could be a target, but her work was involving and satisfying.

And dangerous.

She realized her fingers had crept up to her throat, as if the knife were still there, drawing blood, and for an instant the old memories threatened to swamp her. She fought it down, forced herself to focus on the files in her lap, ordering herself to remember that her job now was to make sure these innocent girls didn't go through anything like what she'd endured.

She would bring them home. Somehow she would bring them home.

Emma parked the ranch truck that had been the only vehicle available to use at the moment, on the main street of Paradise Ridge. Such as it was, she thought; the tiny village made

Eden Falls, population nine hundred, seem like a booming metropolis. If all the tourists left, Emma thought, it would feel like the proverbial wide spot in the road. But the tourists were here, lots of them. Not as many as during the summer, but the holiday shopping season had begun, and many people came here to pick up handcrafted gifts. Most of them were nice and genuinely interested, some just curious, some bordering on being derisive of a culture so foreign to their own and a few just downright rude.

Nice cross section of humanity in general, Emma thought as she got out of the truck and locked it. To protect it from said tourists, since she knew the Amish citizens would never even think of stealing. She supposed there had to be a few bad apples, but they were truly far between.

At least the locals were easy to spot, with their distinctive dress. And while she could hardly ignore the visitors—it was, after all, entirely possible their perpetrator had come here in that guise—for now she would focus on the locals and what they knew or had seen.

The Amish trait of ignoring or spending little time thinking about the foibles of their English neighbors was going to make this difficult. Most of the time the behavior of outsiders truly was ignored as having no import. But what she needed was exactly that, information about anyone who had acted oddly, differently. That this description fit most English to this community wasn't going to help matters.

Emma started to walk, observing, wanting to get the feel of things. This small commercial section of the village had grown a little since she'd last been here, nearly ten years ago. The bakery was still in the same place and still putting out those tempting aromas. A cheese shop had been set up between the bakery and the quilt shop. And beyond that, a flower shop that was full of beautiful, healthy-looking plants.

Everything looked normal. Prosperous.

And yet she felt the tension, barely under the surface. The tourists and shoppers were, naturally, oblivious, but the locals all seemed distracted, as if their thoughts were elsewhere. As she had expected, the abduction of three young girls had traumatized this small community.

She kept walking, looking around. She crossed a narrow alleyway, which, if she recalled correctly, had once marked the end of the small shop area. The next building was a large brick edifice that had, she thought, searching her memory, once been a mill of some kind. But now it appeared only one corner was occupied, remodeled to add a large corner window.

She slowed to a halt before that window. In the top part was, oddly, a birdhouse, she supposed for the martins farmers so prized. But what drew her was the sideboard displayed there. The piece fairly glowed in the late-fall sun, burnished to a smooth, flawless finish, no doubt by hand. Every corner, every angle was perfectly crafted. The wood was rich with grain and clearly selected with care. Each piece mirrored the one before, so that it was clear you were seeing the progression of the tree itself. The overall effect was an incredible melding of nature's symmetry and man's skill.

If there wasn't a good, solid mid-four figures on that price tag, there should be, Emma thought. If not for a closed sign on the door, she'd go in for a closer look. This was the most gorgeous piece of furniture she'd ever seen, and she was already mentally rearranging her apartment to make room for it.

Her gaze shifted, and she realized there was someone in the shop despite the closed sign. A man, in the back, standing near what had to be another window. Probably, she guessed, looking out at the stand of trees to the rear. The sun was at a sharper angle this time of year and poured through that window like a floodlight. It illuminated him as if he were on a stage.

And he could well have been on a stage, for he was a strikingly handsome man. Tall, at least a couple of inches over six feet. Lean, yet well muscled. And the sunlight lit up his features, strong jaw and brow, perfectly cut nose, and a mouth that looked as if it would be softly sensual were it not drawn into a compressed line at that moment. His hair was dark and gleamed in the light streaming over him.

She didn't know how long she just stood there, staring. She wished she had a camera in hand, or that she could draw or paint, for this was a scene worth preserving. Standing there, awash in the soft light of dusk, with that stern, almost pained expression, he stirred feelings in her that she didn't understand yet couldn't deny.

He was as beautiful as the piece in the window, and she knew instinctively he was the maker.

And she had turned into a ridiculous gaping female at the sight of him.

This was *not* a good way to start her investigation.

"May I help you?"

The polite, child-pitched voice had yanked her out of her silly reverie. She had looked down at the child standing beside her, sheepishly aware she hadn't even noticed the girl's approach. Bright blue eyes looked back at her, and she saw dark hair pulled under the traditional head covering.

"This is my father's shop," the girl had explained. "He makes the best furniture in the world."

"Does he?" She couldn't help smiling.

Color stained the girl's cheeks, adding color to the pale porcelain of her skin. "He would never say such a thing—it's vain—but I think I can say it for him."

The simple words had reminded her better than anything else could that she was back among the people who had so fascinated her when she was this child's age.

"And who is your father?"

"Caleb Troyer. He's right in there."

Emma's breath caught. This man, who had so captivated her, who had her standing here in public staring as if she'd never seen a man before, was Caleb Troyer? The brother of the kidnapped Hannah Troyer?

"And you're…?"

"Katie Troyer," the girl said.

The oldest, Emma thought, remembering the file that had said Hannah Troyer had three young nieces through her brother Caleb. And that the girl's mother, Annie Troyer, had died three years ago, leaving Hannah as the main maternal figure in their lives.

"Are you here about my aunt?"

Good guess, or had something given her away?

"What makes you think that?"

"You seem different than the others."

"Different?"

"You dress plainer. More like us than them. Even if you do wear boy's clothes."

Ah, the honesty of children, Emma thought wryly.

"I am from the FBI," she said. At the girl's furrowed brow she added, "We're like the police, only for the whole country."

"Oh. You need my father, then."

That simple statement, Emma thought, opened up a whole new set of crazy thoughts.

This, she thought ruefully, could get complicated.

Chapter 3

"Father?"

Caleb Troyer found it odd that here, where they were alone, Katie would use English. Perhaps it had been to get his attention; he could tell from his daughter's voice that this wasn't the first time she'd called him. With a smothered sigh he slapped his hat against his leg a couple of times, as if the slight blows could shake him out of this mood. He was losing patience with himself, slipping into useless, unproductive states of daydreaming, staring out the windows of his workshop, wasting precious hours that should be spent working.

But how could he work thinking of Hannah,

lively, irrepressible Hannah, out there in the other world, not just in danger of losing her way but having already been grabbed up by the evil that resided there?

Caleb was a strong, competent man, and he'd felt truly helpless only once before in his life. And he couldn't help thinking of that time as helplessness filled him again. He hadn't been able to help Annie as she slipped away after laboring so hard and painfully to bring little Grace into the world three years ago. And there was nothing he could do now.

His instincts were to go himself, to search for his impulsive little sister, but he was wise enough to know he would be useless out there, in that vast expanse that was the world of the outsiders, the English. It was full of technology and other things he knew existed but knew little about. He knew nothing of their huge cities or how to deal with the wickedness that flourished there.

He knew nothing of the kind of person who would do such a thing, take a young, innocent girl off the street for purposes so nefarious Caleb couldn't bear thinking about them. How any man, even an English, could do such things was beyond him.

"Father, please?"

Shaking off the thoughts that had occupied his mind every waking hour since Hannah had been taken, he turned around to face his oldest daughter. As usual, her sweet face both soothed and unsettled him. It was a little easier than it used to be, looking at this beloved child who was such a painful reminder. With her dark hair and blue eyes, she was the living, breathing image of the woman who had been the center of his life since they had been children. The girl he had known he would marry since they had been eleven, the age Katie was now.

Annie had known it, too. When she'd approached him and said "You're the one," he'd known exactly what she'd meant. That someday when they were old enough, they would be together.

"What is it, Katie?" he asked, trying to mask

the sudden tightness in his throat. And again impatience rose in him. He should be worried about his missing little sister, Hannah, not mooning over a woman who'd died three years ago.

"Someone's here."

His mouth quirked at her expression; his already shy daughter looked beyond uneasy. And again his mind shot back to her mother. Annie, too, had been quiet, shy, and only later did he realize what a tremendous certainty she must have had to have approached him that day.

"Deacon Stoltzfus here to chastise me about my beard again?"

The church elder had made it his mission in life to remind Caleb he was going against a basic tenet of Amish life for adult males. As if he didn't know.

He'd grown his beard, as custom dictated, when he'd married Annie. And when she'd died, in a fit of rage and grief, he'd shaved it off, nearly slitting his own throat in the process. His wife had died because of him, trying to deliver his child. And he hadn't been able to save her. He didn't qualify on either front to wear the badge of adult maleness.

So every day he shaved his jaw, those minutes his silent, aching tribute to the woman he missed so much. Without her, he was not a man, and thus he would be without a beard, to the dismay of the entire community.

He waited for Katie to express her usual concern, suggesting he just grow the beard and make the elders happy. Katie was all about making everyone happy, as her mother had been.

"No," the girl said, her voice oddly strained. "It's an English."

Caleb frowned. "Here?"

"A woman." Katie frowned in turn. "She says she's from the...the...some initials."

Initials. That usually meant government. The English had such a need for long, fancy names for their agencies that interfered in the lives of their people.

And then it struck him. Was this about Hannah? Was it some woman from the police? Did

she have news? Why else would she come looking for him, specifically, as Katie had said?

He walked quickly toward the doorway of the
shop. He laid a hand gently on Katie's shoulder
as he went past her.

"Stay here," he commanded and stepped outside into the slanting November sun. Whatever
the woman might say, he doubted he wanted
Katie to hear it. He believed in honesty in what
he said to his children, but that didn't mean they
needed to hear every detail. Selective omission,
Annie had called it, and he'd known there had
been a touch of disapproval in the words. Annie
had been completely, albeit compassionately,
honest. In her way, she had been tougher than
he. She had always found a gentle way to say no
or deliver bad news, whereas he would cringe
inwardly from the task of being harsh with their
girls.

And now it all fell to him.

The sight of the woman waiting outside shook
him out of his pained memories, thankfully rattled him out of his self-pity.

She stood in a shaft of sunlight. And the first thing that struck him was the way that golden light struck her hair, firing it to a luscious blend of colors that matched the fiery fall turning of the leaves. Those leaves were gone now, this first week of November, but her hair brought him the same feeling of wonder at nature's rightness. And the thick richness of it nearly took his breath away. He stopped dead in his tracks.

This was peculiar. Why would her hair affect him like this? It was so unlike Annie's. Her hair had gleamed like a raven's feathers. Of course, he never saw it out in the sunlight like this. She had, as a proper Amish woman, always worn her covering in public. A woman's uncovered hair was for her husband's eyes only, behind closed doors, where such lust-invoking sights belonged.

But for an instant, as he stared at the red, gold and russet, he wanted to touch it, run his fingers through it, see if it felt as warm as it looked.

He yanked his gaze away, angry at himself yet again.

This is why the covering is a good thing, he

lectured himself. And slapped his own hat belatedly on his head.

He realized it was the worry about Hannah that had him off balance. Normally such improper thoughts would have never entered his mind. It had to be that subconsciously he was thinking of his sister's pure red hair, comparing it to this mixture of brown and red and gold that seemed somehow warmer to him. More earthy, as if she were connected to the land, unlike Hannah, whose temperament had always made him fear they would lose her to the outside world.

And now, they had. But not by her choice. The grim reality bit deeply, and he forced himself to focus.

He must have been acting very strangely, for the woman was staring at him. His stomach flipped oddly at the thought that she might have realized his thoughts at the sight of her hair in the sun were not those of a properly raised and trained Amish man. And he could not blame her, not really. For an Englishwoman she was actually very conservatively dressed. Even that hair was, if not under a prayer covering, at least pulled back into a severe style that was less blatant than most. Not that it seemed to lessen the effect, since his second thought after the striking color had been what it would look like down around her shoulders.

But he noticed also that she wore no jewelry, no necklace, no earrings, no rings. He wondered suddenly if she had dressed so, fixed herself so, out of some idea of respecting their traditions or if she was always this unadorned.

And if the absence of a wedding ring, in the English manner, meant she was unattached. Not that it was any of his business. Telling himself firmly the manners and dress of an outsider mattered less than nothing, he walked toward the woman.

"Mr. Troyer?"

Her voice was low, almost husky, and for a moment that quashed reaction threatened anew. For she was closer now, and her eyes were a vivid meadow-green unlike any eyes he'd seen before. That green, plus the reds, golds and browns of her hair… She seemed like some woodland creature, a creature of the earth, the land, who—

He jammed his left hand into his pocket, curling his fingers into a fist, letting his fingernails dig into his flesh. He welcomed the pain; he was obviously out of control with worry, and he needed to focus.

"I am Caleb Troyer," he said formally.

"I'm Emma Colton, with the FBI."

Her voice was brisk as she held up a leather folder with identification. From what he could see from the photograph, she dressed like this regularly. Her hair was even more severely styled, pulled into a knot on her head, tidy except for a few rebellious strands. So she did not use that amazing hair to draw attention to herself. If anything, she seemed to be trying to avoid any acknowledgment that she was female.

Wondering why his usual stern control of his thoughts had deserted him, Caleb tried again.

"You are here about Hannah."

"Yes, sir. I'm from a field office in Ohio,

where, unfortunately, there have been similar cases of Amish girls gone missing."

He nodded. "I was told by the detective from Philadelphia." His dark brows furrowed. "His name is also Colton."

"Tate is my brother."

Caleb's brows rose. "He did not mention that. But you are with the FBI, not the police."

She answered the implicit question with a shrug. "He asked me to come."

"And so you did?"

"Of course."

He liked her answer. Then, his head tilted slightly, he asked, "Then you are Dr. Colton's sister?"

Dr. Derek Colton, whose office was just down the street from the store that sold much of Caleb's handcrafted furniture, was well-known in the Amish community. He was more than generous with his time and care, and seemed to take a special interest in seeing his Amish neighbors stay healthy. He was a good, solid man, and of all the English Caleb dealt with, he thought Derek Colton the most reliable and trustworthy.

"Yes, Derek's my brother," she said. "And before you ask, yes, I'm adopted, too. We all are. All six of us."

She declared it proudly, her love for her family clear in her voice. He liked that.

"I was not going to ask," he said. "Dr. Colton has told me about his family."

He hadn't named them all, however. He'd spoken mostly about their parents and how they all still grieved their loss. He'd found Dr. Colton an honorable and admirable man, but he hadn't made any assumptions about his siblings. He himself was too different from his sister, Hannah, to fall prey to that faulty thinking.

"I didn't come here to talk about my family," she said rather briskly. Indeed, almost sharply, in a sharp, businesslike tone he'd rarely heard from an Amish woman.

"But it is your family, in particular your brother, who has paved your road with his goodwill. If you get cooperation from this community, much of it will be because of him."

"If?" The woman gaped at him. "I'm here to try to find your sister."

"I know this. But don't assume this will automatically ensure trust from all of us."

He was antagonizing her. Purposely.

Caleb realized it with a little jolt. While it was difficult for anyone in the community to turn to outsiders for help, they had all reluctantly agreed this was beyond their scope. Implicit in that was that they would cooperate; they had all agreed with that once the decision had been made.

Including, in fact especially, he himself.

"Then I will find these girls without your help," she said, sounding fierce.

Caleb appreciated her determination. He *wanted* that kind of determination in the search for Hannah. He attempted a fresh start.

"It is difficult for us—"

"What's difficult for me is to understand why anyone wouldn't pull out all the stops to save a child whose life could be in danger."

Caleb wasn't used to being interrupted. Annie would never have dreamed of it. But this woman was clearly nothing like his sweet, retiring Annie. Nothing at all. She was sharp, forceful and very intense.

"I grew up just a couple of miles from here," she said. "And I always had the idea the Amish loved their kids just as we did."

"Of course we do."

"And yet you'll throw roadblocks in the way of the people best equipped to find your missing children?"

Caleb studied her for a long, silent moment. She was indeed fierce, her temper as fiery as her hair in the sunlight. Was it always thus, or was there something specific here that sparked her ire?

"You are very angry," he said.

"Of course I am."

"Anger is an…unproductive emotion."

She stared at him in turn then. "Oh, it can be very productive. Perhaps you could use a little."

"It is not our way."

"Is it your way to stand here and argue with me when your sister is among the missing?"

Caleb gave himself an internal shake. Despite her abrasiveness—well, when compared to Annie anyway—he could not argue with her last point. And he wasn't at all sure why he'd found himself sparring with this woman. She was an Englishwoman, and what they said or did mattered nothing to him.

Except it had to matter now. For Hannah's sake.

Chapter 4

Way to get this started, Emma chided herself.

She had no idea what had gotten into her. She had known perfectly well what she would be facing here, had known that these people wouldn't easily get past the traditions of a lifetime, to hold themselves separate from the outsiders they avoided. Her way, the world's way, wasn't their way, and she'd grown up knowing that. She'd grown up being taught to respect, even when she didn't understand.

And she didn't understand now. Didn't understand how any tradition could be allowed to stand in the way of saving the lives of innocent children.

But that didn't mean she had to take the guy's head off, she thought. She didn't know why she had, why she'd come on so strong and confrontational. She'd learned much better tactics in her career with the FBI, yet it seemed she'd forgotten them all.

Just like she'd forgotten her own name when, caught by the sight of a beautiful sideboard in a display window, she had looked farther into the shop and seen the equally beautiful man standing in the back.

She seized on that. "This is your shop?"

He nodded, looking the slightest bit wary. His eyes were gray, a light, clear color rimmed with a darker edge that made her wonder how they would look at times of high emotion. She cut off her thoughts before she slipped into contemplation of what kind of emotions.

"You built that?" she asked, gesturing at the sideboard in the window.

Again a nod.

"You're…an artist."

One dark brow rose. "I am a carpenter. If there is artistry here, it is God's. He grew the tree."

She blinked. She looked at the piece again, looked at how each board had a mirror image of the grain pattern of the board below it, large at the bottom to smaller at the top, so that it almost looked as if it had been liquid swirled with an unseen brush.

"Point taken," she said.

And for the first time, she saw one corner of his mouth lift in a partial smile.

"But you had the skill, the vision to see the potential," she couldn't resist pointing out.

"And where does my vision come from, if not from God?"

She gave up. The man obviously would not take a simple compliment. But at least they were speaking civilly now, so she could get back to work. And she would begin by yanking her gaze away from that mouth that was indeed as full and sensual as she'd suspected it would be.

He had, she noticed, apparently nicked himself shaving. The small spot of blood on the right line of his jaw was obvious. Somehow that small cut steadied her, kicked her brain back into investigative mode.

It wasn't the only sign of shaving mayhem. There were a couple more nicks, in various stages of healing.

So the man who could use saws and nails and planes and sanders to create this thing of beauty in the window couldn't shave himself without slicing into his own skin? It made no sense to her.

Belatedly, she realized him shaving at all made no sense, not against what she understood of the community he lived in.

"You have no beard," she said.

Any softening she'd seen in him vanished with that simple observation.

"I don't deserve that symbol," he said. His voice was harsh, as if even saying the words were part of some punishment he was bound to endure.

Emma knew Amish men grew their beards—but not mustaches—when they married. In this sect it was a symbol, as he'd said, of that passage to adulthood. She also knew from the file that his wife had died in childbirth three years ago. Did becoming a widower mean the beard had to go? It wasn't as if they could wear black as a sign of mourning—they *always* wore black. The women were allowed some color, if mostly darker shades of blues, greens, browns, but the men seemed to dress mostly in black, sometimes blues.

It was very strange, she thought. She'd grown up seeing the "plain people" all the time; she'd thought nothing of it, didn't find them strange, just different. Her mother had given her a simple explanation of their ways when she'd been a child, and she'd accepted it in the way of a child, been secretly glad she didn't have to wear a dress all the time and thought little more about it than that.

But now, looking at this man, in his simple black trousers, clean, white shirt and suspenders, she found herself picturing what he would look like in the clothing of her world. Put him in a pair of jeans and even that same white shirt, lose the suspenders and the hat, and women would be beating a path to his door.

And she had a sinking feeling she might be first in line.

With an effort larger than she'd had to make in a long while, she forced herself to concentrate on the matter at hand.

"I'm sorry. I didn't mean to intrude on your personal decisions." She tried for a lighter touch. "But you might want to take it a bit easier with that razor."

His hand moved, as if he were going to instinctively touch the fresh cut. But he stopped short, curling his fingers away at the last moment. His hand, she noticed, was strong, well used and marked with a couple of small scars. Yet his fingers were long, graceful, and she glanced at the piece in the window once more. *Artist* definitely applied, she thought.

"That I shave seems everyone's business. How I shave is mine."

There was an edge in his voice. So Mr. Troyer

had a touch of temper, she thought. Or she was seriously rubbing him the wrong way. An awful thought struck her. Was he somehow aware, had he sensed her reaction to him? Had she let it show? Had it been so long since a man, any man, had stirred such interest in her that she wasn't able to hide it even in this most inappropriate of situations?

Or was it simply that he was worried about his sister? That certainly would be enough to put anyone on edge. Although she wondered about that "everyone's business" comment. Wasn't that part of his culture, to play down the individual to maintain the cohesiveness of the community? Yet something was obviously eating at him.

"Why do you shave?" she asked, her curiosity genuine and stemming from a source she didn't care to examine just now. "Is it because your wife died?"

His jaw went rigid. "I do not speak of her to strangers. Especially English."

Then his initial look of shock faded, she guessed as he realized she likely knew more than any stranger would. And she had her answer now; his eyes did indeed darken in moments of emotion. In particular anger.

"I'm sorry," Emma said, knowing she'd crossed a line and uncomfortably aware she'd done it with little justification. She was usually in much better control of herself than this, and she'd better get back to that in a hurry.

"It is enough I have the elders threatening me with sanction, my friends telling me it is time to move on," he muttered.

Then he stopped himself, looking a bit like she felt, as if he were unused to speaking when he didn't mean to. Threat of sanction? For shaving? Was that what he was upset about?

She remembered her father once explaining to her that the Amish, as every human, got angry. But they, unlike too many in the outside world, controlled their anger. They had faith in God's will, and to become angry over something that happened was, to them, to question that will. At the time Emma had been fascinated, but years later a fateful day had made the idea of God's will hard for her to even think about rationally.

But that had no business intruding on what she was here for. Yet something about the way he'd sounded made her say one more thing.

"My parents were killed over a decade ago. I miss them every day of my life. It will never be time to 'move on' if that means forgetting them," she said quietly.

Something flashed in his eyes then, something that seemed almost like gratitude. And when he spoke, there was a note of conciliation in his voice.

"You have questions you wish to ask?"

"You built that birdhouse, too?"

He blinked. "I… Yes." His brows furrowed. "That cannot be what you wanted to ask."

She'd succeeded in throwing him off his guard, at least.

"It's not one of the questions I must ask," she said. "Please understand these are questions that must be asked of everyone, because of the nature of these cases. Many of them you may have already answered to local authorities, but I must ask them again."

"I will tell you everything I can, if it will help you find my sister and her friends."

Those gray eyes watched her steadily, and for a moment she lost track of what she'd intended to say. Which made no sense to her. She was no stranger to powerful men. She was a Colton after all, and it ran in the family. Not to mention the men she worked with. And then there was that little fact of the current resident of 1600 Pennsylvania Avenue being her "Uncle Joe."

Yet none of them had ever made her so addle-headed or disconcerted as this man did.

She cleared her throat and began to ask the questions. For now they were, as she'd said, routine. She and Tate had agreed, before he'd headed back to Philly to pursue that end of the investigation, that it was unlikely that the suspects would come out of the tight-knit Amish community. Not impossible—they were humans like anyone else—but they were held together by their faith and that sense of responsibility for each other that was often lacking outside their society.

As she went through the questions—confirming what she'd read in the file about the date and circumstances of Hannah's disappearance, Hannah's friends and the last to have seen her or them, and adding a few more—Emma's mind was stubbornly gnawing away on other unsettling thoughts. And as she reached the end of the string of standard questions, she reached a rather unsettling, if not downright embarrassing, conclusion.

She had always thought of Amish men differently. It probably stemmed from growing up familiar with them, and the differences between them and the strong, powerful Colton men. She'd spent years watching women fall for brothers, cousins, all of them. She knew what sent them into raptures—although privately she'd been laughing, thinking if they'd grown up with those Colton men they might be singing a very different tune.

By comparison, the Amish men she'd seen so

often as a child had seemed almost another species. Like priests or nuns or monks or anyone else focused on religion. Not less than human, just a different persuasion of human.

Whatever the cause, she'd never had reason to modify that childhood perception, that Amish men were so religious and staid and proper they had little interest in other things. Now that seemed silly. She knew perfectly well the Amish were given to large families, but as an innocent child she hadn't realized the correlation between big families and those…other things. Somehow in her young mind, before she even fully realized what it meant, she'd stuck them with a label of "asexual" and had never revisited the issue.

Until now.

Until as an adult, breathing female, she had to admit what couldn't be denied.

There was nothing, absolutely nothing asexual about Caleb Troyer.

Chapter 5

"Your name is the same as the president's."

There in the middle of the simply furnished room of Caleb Troyer's equally simple but solidly build house, Emma crouched down to look young Ruthie Troyer, Caleb's middle daughter, in the eye. The seven-year-old had a rebellious mane of blond hair that kept escaping what was supposed to be a tidy, plain bun. Her blue-green eyes were fastened on Emma boldly and without fear. Emma guessed from her demeanor, the way she stood and the way she seemed to have only two speeds, stop or full run, that she would be Caleb's biggest handful. In fact, Emma sensed a kindred spirit in the girl and had a strong suspicion that had she been born into the outside world, she would be an irrepressible tomboy.

She felt a pang of sympathy for the girl. How would she herself have survived if not for the indulgence of her family, allowing her to run a bit wild on the ranch, keeping up with the boys and showing little to no interest in learning domestic skills? Eventually she'd learned to cook passably well, but only accepted the lessons because her brothers were forced to learn, as well; there would be no helpless men or women coming out of her house, Charlotte Colton had sternly announced at the start of the summer spent in the big ranch kitchen.

"Yes, my name is the same," Emma said solemnly. "My father was the president's cousin."

The girl didn't look surprised. Perhaps because in her smaller world, the same name often meant a familial connection. Instead, the bright-eyed and obviously smart child fastened on the critical word in what she'd said.

"Was?"

Funny how it could still sting after all these years, Emma thought.

"Yes," she said quietly, sensing that this child, like the girl she herself had been, would see through any dissembling, and then quickly put her in the category of adults who thought you were too young or dumb to understand. "He was killed eleven years ago. Along with my mother."

She wasn't sure if that date that was so infamous in her world registered much in theirs, so she left it at that.

"Both?" Ruthie asked, her eyes widening as she flicked a glance at her own father.

"Yes."

Ruthie absorbed that. And Emma thought she saw the realization dawning in her eyes that bad as losing her mother had been, it could have been worse.

"Eleven years? That's older than me."

"Yes."

"What did they look like?"

She asked it so fiercely Emma was a little taken aback. And then the probable reason for the urgent question struck her, and she answered carefully and in detail.

"My father was like a force of nature. He was tall, about your father's height. He was very strong and handsome. His voice was deep, strong, and when he hugged me and spoke I could feel it booming up out of his chest. He looked a lot younger than he was, with lots of sandy hair and green eyes."

That had always been a comfort to her, that Donovan Colton's eyes had been so like her own that no one would suspect he hadn't been her biological father.

Ruthie was still looking at her, that touch of desperation in her eyes, so she went on.

"My mother was beautiful. Her hair was a bit lighter than yours, and her eyes were just as blue. She was always smiling. Serene, like a warm, sunny day. She could calm a room just by coming into it. They were always there for me, and I still remember and miss them every single day."

Some of the intensity in the girl's posture

ebbed, and Emma saw a touch of relief in her eyes.

"Just as you will always remember your mother, even when you are old and gray," she added softly, knowing she'd read the girl who reminded her of herself correctly.

"Ruthie." Caleb's own deep voice seemed tense as he interrupted. "Go gather your little sister from Mrs. Stoltzfus."

The child hesitated, her gaze flicking to Emma as if she were reluctant. But only for a moment, then she quickly went to obey her father, so quickly Emma wondered if that undertone in his voice was more than simply sternness, if Caleb was so strict with his children that they dare not even protest an unwanted command.

For a command it had been, there was no doubt about that, she thought as she straightened up. She knew Amish men were the undisputed heads of their house, but she'd always thought their women were a quiet power behind closed doors. But perhaps they were not; perhaps they were completely submissive, dutiful. And she—

Emma interrupted her own thoughts as the idea struck that perhaps it was not his daughter Caleb Troyer was tense about. Perhaps it was her.

She swiftly reviewed what she'd said to the child and found nothing that could provoke such a response. She hadn't even really asked the girl any pertinent questions other than if she'd spoken to her aunt the day she'd vanished, if Hannah had said anything unusual to her. She would want to talk to the girl in more detail later, but right now her focus had been on getting the child to trust her a little. And she thought she'd done that, by sharing her own painful memories, and—

"I never realized," Caleb said.

She turned to look at him then. He was rubbing his jaw, and one glance at his face told her the person he was upset at was himself.

"Realized what?" she asked, a little startled at the relief she felt that he wasn't angry at her.

"That she was afraid of forgetting what her mother looked like."

"It's only natural. And," she added honestly, "perhaps more difficult in your culture, because there are few photographs."

"We do not believe in images."

"I know. I'm not criticizing, just saying it makes it harder at times like this. Then again, perhaps always seeing a picture on the wall as a reminder of your loss—or taking it down and finding it makes no difference, because you simply always notice it's gone and remember why— is even harder."

Caleb stared at her for a long, silent moment. "You are…not what I expected a person from the FBI to be."

"Human, you mean?" She smiled when she said it, determined not to return to that confrontational demeanor.

"Caring," he said. "I would think, with the work you do, you would avoid that."

"They do their best to train it out of you," she admitted. "They know it drains you, sends you on the way to burnout faster."

She didn't mention that this training hadn't

taken very well with her. She always struggled to maintain that detachment, her natural empathy becoming both a strength and a weakness. This was something she barely even admitted to herself, because then she'd have to admit they were right. After seven years she was already closer to burnout than some of her colleagues who had been around twice as long.

"And yet you care about the feelings of a child who has lost her mother."

"That doesn't have anything to do with this case."

"And you have felt this pain yourself."

She was uncomfortable with his steady regard and with the personal turn this had taken. She had opened that door herself, however, with Ruthie, so she could hardly complain about it now.

"I have. I do."

"Eleven years?"

"I'll still feel it after fifty," she said, almost defiantly, wondering if he was one of those who would tell her it was time to get over it.

"You will," he agreed quietly, startling her. And then she silently chided herself. Ruthie had lost her mother, but this man had lost his wife. "That was not what I meant. Eleven years ago was 2001."

"Yes."

"And you lost them both, together."

"Yes."

He seemed to hesitate for a moment, then, his deep voice soft, he said rather than asked it, as if he already knew the answer. "September 11."

"Yes." She studied him for a moment. "I wasn't sure how much impact that had in the Amish community."

His mouth tightened slightly. "It had tremendous impact. It tested our beliefs like few things ever have. And our relationship with you English."

She'd never really thought about it, not from their point of view. "You mean because you don't believe in fighting back."

"And we were often held in contempt for it. We

love our country, but because our beliefs forbid flying its flag it was assumed we did not."

"You don't fly the flag because of your beliefs," she said slowly, almost wonderingly, "but how do you decide to remain a pacifist in the face of people who kill us in the name of theirs?"

"It is not a decision, Agent Colton. It is who we are."

They had proven that, time and again, so she didn't see any use in arguing the point.

"Sometimes," she said, her gaze unfocused as she remembered the horrors of that day, "I envy you the simplicity and peace of your lives."

"Many do," he said. "But few are truly willing to do what it takes to attain it."

She refocused abruptly. He was looking at her with a mild sort of amusement. She supposed he had heard that often from visitors or tourists who enthused about their way of life until the realization came that they really would have to give up so much of what they took for granted.

"You are truly related to the English president?"

"He's your president, too. But yes. I grew up calling him Uncle Joe."

"He seems a good man."

"He is. He's already done some good things."

"I know little of that," Caleb said. "But unlike others, he's done nothing of harm to us."

Again Emma felt a pang; what must it be like to only have to judge a small portion of what craziness went on in the world, the small portion that directly affected you and yours? The idea of not having to thrash her way through all the complications and political gamesmanship that made her life an occasional morass was beyond tempting. It was like Shangri-la, something she longed for but wasn't sure really existed.

"Ruthie's mother," she began, then stopped, unable to think how to phrase a question that had nothing to do with why she was here.

Caleb went very still. His mouth tightened, and his voice became rough. "I do not speak of her to my family. I certainly will not speak of her to a stranger. She has nothing to do with this."

The words and his tone were harsh, but Emma

had had enough training and practice in reading people to realize they both were outward evidence of a powerful inward emotion.

The man had loved his wife. Enough, apparently, to risk sanction from his church, she thought as she looked again at the nick that marred his strong, smooth-shaven jaw. She wondered how long the elders' patience would last, how much slack they would give a grieving widower before they took action. Would they really do something like shun him for shaving that Amish symbol of manhood, the beard, when it was done out of grief?

I don't deserve that symbol.

His words echoed in her head. The harsh tone echoed what she had just heard from him. It had sounded like more than simple grief. And with a sudden flash of insight she thought she knew why. She knew because it was a trait every Colton man had in spades.

You protected your own.

And if you failed at that, you weren't a Colton. You weren't even really a man.

She was familiar with the mind-set.

She admired the mind-set, for the most part.

She'd just never expected to find it here. She'd thought it bred out of these men, long ago, through submission to what they saw as the will of God.

In a way, it relieved her. It took her a while to realize why.

It meant Caleb Troyer wasn't quite perfect after all.

Chapter 6

Sometimes, Caleb thought, he would like nothing more than to walk away. As he sat in his chair next to the gas lamp, a book open in his lap but so far unread, he imagined a life without the constant reminders, a life not lived in the house he and Annie had shared. A life where everyday things didn't jab at him, seeming to taunt him with the loss of the sweet, shy woman who had loved him with all her heart. And whom he had loved since the moment he'd first seen her.

Something the Englishwoman had said went through his mind, about taking down pictures of a loved one who had passed.

...and finding it makes no difference, because

you simply always notice it's gone and remember why...

Would it truly be that way somewhere else, away from all the reminders? Was it not the reminders at all, but something missing inside himself? Had Annie truly taken his heart with her, was that why he felt so hollow?

He felt a flash of anger that he immediately quashed with the ease of long practice. He had no right to feel anger at what had clearly been God's will. Annie had died in the most natural of acts, bringing a child into the world. If anyone deserved anger it was he himself. He should have called for Dr. Colton sooner, the moment things had started to go wrong. Even though he'd come immediately, arriving much more quickly than Caleb would have thought possible, by the time he did get there Annie was lying still and lifeless.

Dr. Colton. A fine man, a good man, and a good doctor. And he was the FBI woman's brother. This woman who had obviously gained wisdom from her own tragedy. Because deep inside he knew she was right. Leaving his home would not cure the pain he felt. The hollowness was not in a place or a building. It was in him.

He chided himself sharply; he had no time for self-pity or worse, dwelling on the words, however wise, of a woman not of his world. And yet he found himself staring at the rack on the wall by the door where Annie's cape had always hung, empty now, and the simple truth in what she had said struck home.

"Father?"

Katie's voice was hesitant, so much like her mother's it felt like a punch to his stomach every time she spoke. But especially when he was lost in this kind of self-indulgent musing.

"Katie," he acknowledged.

"I'm through with my schoolwork. May I read my book before bedtime?"

"Yes."

The girl was deep into a series of novels about quilting that she had begun reading with her mother. She'd only recently begun to read them again. For over a year after Annie's death, Katie had wanted nothing to do with them. She had stuffed them into the corner of the dresser Caleb had built for her before she was born, covering them with folded aprons and caps, as if putting them out of sight would make—

And as quickly as that he was back to the words of the FBI woman.

"Father," Ruthie began.

"Schoolwork," he answered, knowing her well enough that she wouldn't be finished yet. Ruthie was bright, clever and quick, but was also easily distracted. A simple school essay could take hours because she would veer down a side path she found irresistibly fascinating.

Grace, thankfully, was sound asleep tucked in her small bed in the girls' room. Next year, when she turned twelve, Katie would move to her own room. She could have had it much earlier, but after her mother's death, she had clung to Ruthie and new baby Grace, and he hadn't had the heart to part them. But the room they all shared was crowded, and it was silly to continue the practice when there were four empty bedrooms in the house. Hannah had told him it was past time Katie had her own room and she would soon need privacy.

A shiver went through him. Hannah loved her nieces and was always ready to lend a hand. In fact, she got more cooperation out of them than he sometimes could; her irrepressible spirit and her sense of humor usually had them laughingly complying with even the most onerous of tasks.

He didn't know what he'd do without her.

He shifted his gaze to the two heads bent over the table, Katie reading intently, Ruthie scribbling words with a speed that had him thinking he'd be needing to check that paper before she handed it in.

His girls. He loved them dearly, not just for their own sakes, but because they were all he had left of Annie. And he realized with thudding finality that he would never leave Paradise Ridge. He would never start over somewhere else, because it would mean ripping his children away from their only remaining solace, the loving support of the community. Every female in the village pitched in to help him with the girls. And if some of them, as Mrs. Yoder had warned, had eyes on filling Annie's shoes, well, that just wasn't going to happen.

No, he would not be going anywhere. Even if he could tolerate the change himself, it would be too cruel to uproot the girls, whose lives had already been turned upside down, just because he wished he could escape.

There would be no escape.

Emma stopped on the path to Caleb Troyer's house. Even in the fading light of dusk, the details were clear: the stone foundation, the covered porch that ran the width of the house, the evenly spaced windows. Smoke curled out of the chimney, a homey touch she hadn't realized she'd missed until she saw it now. It was a simple house, as were all Amish homes, but it looked solid and well built. But she supposed a carpenter as skillful as Caleb would settle for nothing less.

One of those windows by the front door glowed

with light, and as she walked up the steps to the porch, she could see into the front room of the house. She paused on the top step. She could see the woodstove on one wall, obviously in use in this brisk almost-winter weather. But what caught her eye was the table before it, where two young girls sat in the surprisingly bright light of what appeared to be a gas lamp. Their heads were bent, one over a book she was reading intently, the other over papers spread on the table, one of which she was writing on with a tightly clutched pencil.

Something about the simple tableau tightened her throat. She felt a yearning that startled her with its power, especially since she couldn't even put a name to what she was yearning for.

She was happy enough in Cleveland. Her work was rewarding, if a bit routine, something that would surprise most whose idea of the FBI came from film or television.

Caleb wouldn't have those ideas, she thought suddenly. Because he wouldn't have been influenced by either of those things. Most times when she thought of life without the technology everyone relied on, it was with a wondering shake of her head. When people learned she had grown up in Amish country, they were often full of questions, mostly about how some people could stand to live like that. Her standard answer had always been that you don't miss what you've never had.

But now she wasn't so sure they weren't better off without the pervasive hammering of popular culture and the twenty-four-hour news cycle. The idea of simply unplugging held a lot more appeal than it once had.

She gave herself a mental shake. She'd expected to feel at home here in this countryside she'd grown up in, but she hadn't expected this wave of…what was it, homesickness? How could you feel homesick when you were, essentially, at home?

"Because you know you're not staying," she muttered as she took that last step onto the porch. It was as solidly built as the rest of the house, the boards beneath her feet feeling even and level.

In size and layout, it appeared to match most of the houses here in Paradise Ridge, yet it was different, because instead of the traditional and ubiquitous white paint, it was finished with a clear coat of some kind—

The front door swung open. Caleb Troyer stood there, limned from behind in golden light. She was struck again by how tall he was. Struck by how lean he was. Struck by the strength of his jaw, the structure of his face.

Struck dumb, apparently, she thought when she realized he'd been looking at her in polite inquiry for several seconds.

"Miss Colton?" he finally said.

She said the first thing that popped into her head. "Your house isn't white."

His brows rose. "You came here to tell me this?"

She felt beyond foolish. She'd interviewed terrorists, serial killers, kidnappers, yet she couldn't seem to get her mind and her mouth in sync around this man.

"I was just wondering why."

"My father built this house. It's what he did, build houses. Not just here, but for outsiders, as well. He kept this house this way, with no paint to disguise any flaws, as an advertisement."

"That's allowed?"

His mouth quirked, and she wondered if she were going to get some kind of lecture about asking impertinent or intrusive questions that had nothing to do with why she was here. She told herself that was part of the job, too, to build a rapport of sorts, but she wasn't convincing herself.

"Many things are allowed," he said, in a tone she guessed he probably used to explain things to his children, "if they can be shown to have a good purpose and not to be harmful to the community."

"It's…beautiful," she said, somehow stung by that tone, although she thought she hid it well enough.

"I believe what sold the bishop was my father's argument that showing the natural state of the wood, which is God's design, could hardly be a bad thing."

Emma blinked. His tone had changed completely, was now warmer, as if sharing a confidence. As, perhaps, he was. It seemed to her a very clever argument.

"Your father was a smart man."

"He was." She thought he smothered a sigh. "Smarter than I, certainly."

"Are you going to invite her inside out of the cold, Father?"

It was Katie who'd spoken. The girl had moved so quietly even her father seemed startled when she spoke practically from beside his elbow. Emma, facing the room, had seen the movement but said nothing. Watching the natural interaction of a family involved in a crisis like this one was often very illuminating.

To her amazement, Caleb flushed slightly. "Of course," he said, his voice gruff but not angry. Embarrassed, perhaps, at being reminded of his manners by his eleven-year-old daughter?

"Come in," he said, backing up and holding the door open.

She stepped inside. The room was as warm and cozy as it had looked through the window. As with all Amish homes, it was simply furnished. Yet each wood chair, the storage pieces along the walls and the table the girls had been sitting at bore the signs of that fine craftsmanship she'd seen in his shopwindow earlier. The lines were simple, unadorned in the Amish way, but the quality shone through. She guessed those chairs would be as solid in twenty years as they were now.

Ruthie abandoned any pretense at concentrating on what appeared to be schoolwork on the table before her, got up and approached them.

"Aren't you supposed to be looking for Aunt Hannah?"

"Ruth," Caleb said sternly, "don't be rude."

Emma couldn't help smiling. "I don't blame her for asking. But let me ask you something, Ruthie. If I told you I'd lost something outside and asked you to help me find it, what would you do?"

"I would help you. That's what people do."

Emma felt a small jab. If that were always true, life would be so much simpler. But then, that's what the Amish were all about, wasn't it—a simpler life?

"So, we go outside, and then what?"

"We would look," the girl said, brows furrowing. Emma had the distinct impression she was thinking something about how silly this grown-up was.

"Where?"

"Where you were when you lost it," the girl said with an air of strained patience.

"And how would you know where that was?"

Ruthie sighed, as if her patience had run out. "I'd ask you."

Emma sensed she was a very bright girl, and so she simply waited, saying nothing more. For an instant her gaze flicked to Caleb, who had subsided into silence and was watching intently.

It didn't take the girl long. Her furrowed brow was cleared by dawning realization.

"You mean that's what you're doing? Finding out where to look?"

"Exactly."

"Oh."

The child appeared satisfied, and Katie smiled at her. Caleb said nothing to her, but directed Ruthie to finish her schoolwork and spoke to Katie about putting away clothing.

"Mrs. Stoltzfus's daughter was kind enough to wash them. You should honor that by taking proper care."

Something flashed in the girl's blue eyes, but she only said "Yes, Father" and disappeared through a doorway at the back of the room.

The girl knew, Emma realized.

If there was one thing Emma had learned today in her preliminary interviews with a few of the residents of the village and the surrounding farms, it was that Caleb Troyer was on the figurative radar of every unmarried woman around.

It might well be that it was that sense of intense community that Amish life fostered brought on much of the generous help he was given, help with the girls and with the chores commonly relegated to the female domain, but it hadn't taken Emma long to figure out that many of those women also had an eye on stepping into his late wife's shoes.

Not that she didn't understand perfectly. She was, after all, the one who had gone all wobbly the moment she'd spotted him standing in the back of his shop.

But Caleb seemed oblivious to their interest, much to their sorrow.

And to her own relief.

Chapter 7

"Thank you for your patience with my daughter." Caleb sounded formal, almost stiff.

"She reminds me of me, at that age," Emma said.

She saw a touch of alarm flash through his eyes at her words. It stung, a lot more than it should have. He was, after all, only part of this case. He was the brother of one of the victims, no more.

That he was also the first man in aeons who sent her pulse racing didn't matter. Couldn't be allowed to matter. He was Amish, for God's sake.

The irony of her own thoughts made her laugh

inwardly, and the sting vanished in a rush of awareness of the absurdity of it all. She might long to return to the quiet life at the ranch—a realization that had surprised her with its power the moment they'd gone through the gates—but Amish life was something else again. She might long for some simplicity and quiet, but that would require sacrifice, dedication and change she didn't think she was capable of.

"Don't worry," she said wryly. "I'm sure she'll get over it."

He had the grace to look abashed. "I did not mean—"

"It's all right. I've spent the day talking to many of the women in the community, and I understand perfectly what you mean. A woman like me would never fit in here," she said as she took the seat he indicated, a simple upholstered chair that, while not the big, overstuffed style in the ranch house great room, was surprisingly comfortable.

She took a quick glance around the room, observing in the way she had been trained to. Ironic that this simple, plain house was furnished with pieces, all showing that same fine hand, that would bring high prices in the outside world, yet here they were merely functional.

Against the wall beside her was a bookshelf, and she saw it was full of a varied collection—history, biographies, classic novels—and on the lower shelves children's classics, including the *Little House* books she'd known in her own childhood. No modern thrillers or ripped-from-the-headlines stuff, but she wouldn't have expected that, not here in this world that until now was so removed from outside cares and fears.

There was nothing here that would be in the least out of place in any Amish home, nothing to indicate any break with the constraints of the community.

"A woman like you are now," he amended her words, surprising her.

"You really think a person could change? That much?"

"With God's help, all things are possible."

She had the oddest feeling the words were spoken by rote. They were what was supposed to be said to such questions, so he said them.

"What about when God doesn't help?"

He stiffened. "It is not for us to question his will."

He said it like a mantra, and she wondered how many times he'd chanted it after the death of his wife. By all accounts—and the women had made it clear, by implication and in so many words—he had loved his wife dearly. Childhood sweethearts since they had been Katie's age. Emma was more than a little in awe of that kind of bond. Her own romantic life had been scattered, often falling victim to her career and her drive to succeed, to prove herself so that nobody could ever again accuse her of having made it on the Colton name.

"What is it you wished to ask?"

"I need to speak to the girls."

"You mean about their aunt."

She wondered if he called Hannah their aunt because it was somehow less painful than saying "my sister."

"Yes."

"I've already spoken to them. They know nothing about her disappearance. They were not at the barn party."

Emma nodded. She knew this; the barn party Hannah and her friends Miriam and Rebecca were taken from had been part of the *rumspringa* and not for younger children.

"I understand," she said. "But I still need to speak to them. I know their aunt was very close to them. Perhaps she said something that might help the investigation. Or they may have heard something."

"They would have told me."

"They may not realize they've heard something important. They're children, and sometimes people say things around them they ordinarily wouldn't, because they mistakenly think they are too young to understand."

Caleb's gaze flicked to Ruthie, and Emma guessed her words had proven true with the clever girl more than once.

"You may speak to them," he finally agreed.

Emma braced herself. "Alone," she said.

Again he stiffened. "No. I will be there."

"Sometimes," Emma said, trying to pick her words carefully, "children don't speak as freely if a parent is in the room."

"My daughters answer whatever questions I ask them."

"I don't doubt that. But there's a difference between answering questions and volunteering information."

He frowned. "You believe they know something they haven't told?"

"I only know that, in my experience, children often do."

"But if they were not there—"

Emma drew on her dwindling store of patience; in a strange way this was like dealing with a gang-related crime. Maybe even worse, because nobody knew how to close ranks like the Amish.

"Hannah may have said something to one of them. Something that might give us a clue."

She saw realization dawn in his eyes. Caleb Troyer was no slouch, either.

"Do you believe she was not taken? That she left of her own will?"

"That is a possibility we have to consider."

Slowly, Caleb shook his head. "Why would she sneak away? It was her *rumspringa*. She was free to leave if she wished."

"Perhaps she was afraid people would try to talk her out of it."

"Our children are given great leeway during this time. Of course, we do not support doing anything against our basic beliefs, but exploration is expected. She would have no reason to hide it."

"I understand but—"

"And she most assuredly would not leave without talking to the girls. They are very close."

"Exactly," Emma said softly.

She didn't push, didn't press, sensing that this man would make up his mind in his own good time, and trusting that he would see the reason in what she'd said, and the conclusion he himself had reached.

After a moment he gave a sharp nod. "You may speak to them."

Together, the girls appeared touchingly innocent to her. Even the feisty Ruthie seemed calmer in the presence of her quietly lovely older sister. She spoke to them together, then separately, and when she was done she was as certain as she could be that they knew nothing about their aunt's disappearance.

She watched as, after a single announcement of "Time, girls" from Caleb, the two gathered their things and put them neatly away, and went about preparing for bed obediently. She smothered a wry smile as she remembered the battles at home getting Piper and Sawyer to go to bed. Perhaps these people were onto something here.

"They're very…cooperative," she said.

"They know they must get up early. There are many chores before school."

While she and her siblings all had had their assigned duties at the ranch, they were generally expected after school. She should have been more thankful, she thought now, remembering her own struggles to get up and get moving in the mornings back then. Now, with frequent early callouts to deal with some incident that occurred during the night, it was as if her body clock had been reset, and rising early had become the norm.

Well, not quite as early as this morning, when her brother's call had blasted her awake, she thought with a grimace.

"You think we are too hard on our children?" he asked.

Startled, she shifted her gaze to him. "No. In fact, I think we on the outside could learn a thing or two from you. Our kids get into a lot more trouble than yours."

"Your world invites it," he said.

"Relatively speaking, I can't deny that."

He seemed surprised by her admission.

"Don't you hear that a lot, from the tourists? That they admire your simple life?"

"Yes," he said. "Some even wish to join us.

They are looking for something here that they should be looking for within themselves. This is why we call them seekers."

"Seekers?"

He nodded. "The problem is that they do not realize that simple does not necessarily mean easy."

There was a lot of wisdom in those words, she thought. But then, she'd been raised knowing that the path these people trod was not easy. But to them, rewarding in a way few outside could understand.

A sudden memory came to her, and she smiled.

"I remember once when my parents were particularly exasperated with me, they threatened to send me to spend the summer with an Amish family. At the time, the very idea of doing without my computer or my music player or my cell phone struck terror into my heart."

"At the time?" he asked.

She nodded, wondering why he'd seized on that out of all she'd said. "Yes. Now I see the appeal."

He looked at her so thoughtfully it made her uneasy. But then, just having those eyes focused on her, just having this man's full attention, made her uneasy.

"You deal with the worst ugliness in an ugly world," he said finally. "How do you keep it from polluting your very soul?"

Something about the tone of his voice, as if he were actually feeling pain for her, moved her deep inside in a way she'd never known before. "Sometimes," she said, "you don't."

Memories rose up in a swamping tide, vicious memories uglier than anything a man like Caleb Troyer could imagine. She'd been warned by the agency shrink that despite her every effort, they would break through now and then, and that she must accept that she had been traumatized and that there would be aftereffects.

"Agent Colton? Are you well?"

She gave herself a fierce mental shake. "I'm fine."

But she was not. She could feel that tonight the images were not going to be simply quashed as usual. Tonight, they were going to win, and she had a rocky road ahead of her for the next few hours.

"Thank you for letting me speak to the girls," she said formally, trying desperately to hold on.

He didn't remind her that he'd told her she would learn nothing, and she appreciated that. Especially just now. "Yes. Are you all right? You look ill."

"I'm fine," she said quickly, almost desperately, as if saying it could make it true.

"You are not," he said bluntly. "What is wrong? Is it something you've learned? Something about Hannah?"

"No. No, I'm sorry." It was gaining on her, rapidly.

His voice changed then, became softer, more gentle. And it almost undid her. "Tell me what's wrong. What can I do?"

"Nothing," she whispered.

She made some sort of mumbled excuse and fled. And *fled* was the word for it; at that moment she wanted away from that man more than she wanted to keep breathing. It wasn't until she was pulling through the ranch gates that she confronted the truth that had been driving her.

She didn't want Caleb Troyer to know what had happened to her.

The agency knew, her coworkers obviously knew, since it had happened in the line of duty. Her family knew, although Derek and Tate were the only ones who knew the whole of it. Tate had found out through his connections as a cop, and Derek had demanded the full truth from her as a doctor as well as her brother.

She didn't understand this. Not the hammering of the images, the torturing of her mind, the pain of her body in this moment as real as it had been then; she had come to expect it and viewed progress as the fact that it happened less and less often. But even that hope was undermined by her silent, unconfessed fear that the shrink hadn't certified her okay for duty because she truly was, but because her last name was Colton. Fear that she truly wasn't mentally strong enough for her job, even after two years.

But she understood all that, she wrestled with it daily. What she didn't understand was why she had just been nearly torn in two by the need to keep Caleb from ever finding out and the need to pour it all out to him.

He might be one of the most quietly strong men she'd ever met, but the kind of evil she'd confronted was foreign to him.

She didn't want him to know she'd been abducted and held by a brutal serial rapist for nine horrifying days. She didn't want him to know how frightened she'd been, afraid she would die…and then afraid she would not.

…how do you keep it from polluting your very soul?

She didn't want this devout, moral man to know that she was very much afraid she'd lost her soul.

Chapter 8

Gunnar would understand, she thought as her headlights lit the narrow road that led to his cabin on the most remote part of the ranch. He understood about memories that wouldn't leave you alone. Her big, strong brother had come home from the Middle East a changed man. A tortured man they all worried about.

He could use some of that Amish peace, she thought.

But for that very reason, she didn't feel she could or should turn to him. She was a little afraid of what might happen if they took their individual hauntings and rubbed them together.

So she drove on past, heading for the big, main ranch house.

She could see the stable off to her left. She felt a sudden urge for a long ride—and a pulse-pounding run—across the ranch's open reaches. Maybe she'd have to make time for that. It would do wonders to settle her suddenly tangled emotions. In fact, perhaps she'd even ride to Paradise Ridge from here once or twice.

She liked the idea. Every Amish home and shop had a hitching post anyway; surely they wouldn't mind if she showed up on a horse.

Of course, if she had to go in pursuit of a car for some reason, she'd have some explaining to do. There was that.

She'd managed to make herself smile, feeling calmer as she made the last turn and the big house spread out before her.

Home.

For a long moment after she parked, she just sat there, looking at it. She had grown up here, knowing every day how lucky she was. Shortly after their parents' deaths, she and her siblings had gathered here in a shocked numbness that would soon turn to anger. Their emotions were raw, and their reactions ranged from wanting to sell the ranch to be rid of the reminders of what they'd lost, to wanting to hole up there as a family and never set foot in the outside world again.

In the end, it was Derek's choice to make, for their parents had left the decision making in the hands of the most levelheaded and responsible of the six of them. Even at a young age it was clear that Derek was their rock, the unwavering core that held them all together. He'd only been in his early twenties at the time of the September attack, but that they were still together as a family and the ranch still prospered was a testament to the wisdom of Donovan and Charlotte Colton's decision.

She needed to give her brother a big hug next time she saw him.

The front door popped open, light from the entryway spilling out onto the large covered porch.

"Hey! It's the feds!"

Emma rolled her eyes at her baby brother, even though he couldn't see her from here. Sawyer Colton was full of sass for his family—especially his long-suffering sister Piper—and yet at the same time the boy was deeply thoughtful and sometimes surprised them all with the ideas he came up with after long contemplation of something new.

She was grinning at him when she got out of the car. He'd been in school when she'd arrived so this was the first she'd seen him. Sawyer flew at her, and she braced herself for the slam of his agile little body and his fierce hug. She didn't mind; she was glad he was still young enough to want to hug his big sister.

"A little respect," she said with mock severity as she hugged him back. "That's federal agent to you."

"Yeah, yeah," Sawyer said with a laugh.

"I thought you wanted to be one of us," she said. "Or is it back to doctor this week?" She knew Sawyer idolized Derek and hung around the clinic often after school. But he also idolized

Tate and, she admitted, her, and wanted to be in law enforcement.

"I've decided I want to be both. A doctor and a cop."

Emma laughed. "Hey, I could use a medical examiner in the family. And if anybody's got the energy to do both, you do, bro."

"And I wish he'd burn more of it off at school and give us a break."

The wry words came from the doorway. Emma turned and smiled at the sight of her little sister. *Little* being a chronological reference only, since Piper at sixteen was already two inches taller than Emma's own five-seven. Taller, and impossibly blonde with bright blue eyes. She looked as if she'd walked out of an advertisement for travel to Scandinavia. And woe be unto the unwary person who thought blonde meant dumb; Piper was wise well beyond her years and would make mincemeat of anyone who assumed otherwise.

"Hi, sis," Emma said with a smile as Sawyer made a snorting sound at his closest sibling. As the baby of the family, he had no one younger to pick on, so tried to make up for it by aiming with regularity at the only Colton still living at home with him, Piper. Piper, in turn, often retreated to Derek's ranch house for respite, or Gunnar's more remote cabin if Sawyer was in particularly rare form.

"You're home late. Any progress?" Piper asked. News of the abductions had spread rapidly from Paradise Ridge through the small town of Eden Falls, and Piper was concerned. Not simply because the girls were near her own age, but because she was by nature a generous soul and worried about the plights of others. As they all were.

Emma wondered, not for the first time, if her parents had had some sort of special radar that told them which of the kids they encountered had that same sort of urge to help that they themselves had. Because they all had it, in one form or another. How it would manifest in these youngest two remained to be seen, but Emma had no doubt that it would.

"Just getting the lay of the land, as it were.

Talked to the families." An image of Caleb Troyer shot through her mind, unbidden. And a responding heat shot through her body, and she groaned inwardly. This *had* to stop.

"And the church leaders." She made herself go on. "They're calling a meeting in the schoolhouse tomorrow so I can talk to everyone. Then I'll start digging in."

"They shouldn't have waited so long," Sawyer said.

"It would be easier if they hadn't," Emma agreed. "Evidence and leads are easier to find and follow when they're fresh."

"Not a cold case, you mean," Sawyer said.

"Gotta love TV," Emma said. Then she added, before Sawyer got set in the idea he was in a position to judge, "The Amish are used to handling things themselves. It's as hard for them to ask for outside help as it is for you to quit teasing Piper."

Sawyer looked appropriately sheepish. "Yeah, yeah," he said again. "C'mon, dinner's ready. Margie was about to serve up without you."

The boy darted back inside. Emma turned to follow, only to find Piper studying her intently with those cornflower-blue eyes.

"What's wrong? Besides the case, I mean."

In addition to the Nordic looks and generous heart, Piper was also very perceptive. But explaining that she was distracted beyond belief by the brother of one of her victims, a man she had no business even thinking about, was something she wasn't about to share with her sixteen-year-old sister.

"It's just a tricky community to work with," she said.

"But you've always admired them."

Perceptive indeed, especially since Piper was thirteen years younger than she and had been barely six when Emma had headed off to college. But she'd come home at every possible school break and every summer, and as her little sister grew older, that perceptiveness grew with her.

"Sometimes," Emma said wryly, "I even envy them."

Piper grimaced, her face full of a teenager's

horror at the thought of giving up her electronics. She was glued to her music player as often as Sawyer was glued to his game console, playing the latest in some series of exceptionally noisy video games. She'd be worried about the violence of it if he didn't also immediately ask to borrow her phone to play with those silly birds and pigs and get just as excited.

"Dinner is ready," Piper said. "We should go in. I don't want Margie mad at me, or we'll have brussels sprouts for a week."

"Shiver," Emma said with a laugh and followed her sister inside.

Margie had been their part-time cook and housekeeper since Derek had sent her home, pulling her out of an abusive relationship that had gone on for years. She wasn't the first patient her brother had sent home to work at the Double C, and Emma doubted she would be the last. And Margie was a prize; the woman could turn the simplest of ingredients into the best-tasting dishes. She'd always said Emma had the knack, too. But the interest was lacking, Emma knew, and she too often ate out or on the run.

Except for the occasional drop-in by an adult Colton hungry for her cooking, Margie had only the younger kids to worry about now, and herself and Julia, the nanny who had helped raise all six Coltons and was still there part-time for Piper and Sawyer. Both women, considered part of the family, would be welcome even if there was no one left to cook for or care for.

After a meal that blatantly featured her favorite dishes, lots of chatter from Piper and Sawyer, a phone call from Derek welcoming her home and promising to see her soon—Gunnar, as usual, remained his reclusive self—and a message from Tate that he was back in Philly pursuing what was probably another dead end, Emma retreated to her room to try and get some rest so she could begin fresh in the morning.

It wasn't going to be easy. There was too much rolling around in her mind—being back home, catching up with everyone. Enough to keep anybody whirling.

"Right," she muttered to herself as she finished brushing her teeth and climbed into her wonderfully familiar bed. "That's all it is, just the usual chaos on the home front."

As she sat there looking around at her room, which was much as it had been when she'd gone off to college, she even almost convinced herself it was just a normal day in the Colton house, a bit crazed. That's all.

When her gaze fell on the family photograph that hung in a spot of honor, as it did in all the kids' rooms in this house, whether still occupied or not, she felt the usual stab of sharp agony, not at all dulled by time, only shorter in duration. And as always, her eyes focused on the beautiful couple at the center of the array: Donovan Colton, tall, lean, with his rakish grin, and Charlotte beside him, her blond hair windblown, her smile serene and happy, baby Sawyer in her arms.

It was the last photo taken of them all together, just after Sawyer had come to them. And just before that September day that had nearly destroyed them.

She turned out the light and lay back against the pillows, although the image was still clear in her mind's eye. She was luckier than the kids had been; she'd had their parents until adulthood at least. She just wasn't feeling lucky right now.

She was feeling confused.

And just like that, Caleb Troyer was back in her thoughts. In a way he reminded her of her father; not in looks, but in the competence he exuded under the handsome exterior. She'd learned that Caleb was considered the best carpenter and furniture builder in the entire county, and that his pieces sold for amazing prices to the English, or outsiders. Her father would have appreciated that. He had appreciated anyone who was the best at what he did.

But what she felt when she looked at Caleb, what she felt when she was close to him, when he turned those steady eyes on her, was anything but familial.

And that, she told herself sternly as she

pounded her pillow into shape with more enthusiasm than was really necessary, was something she was just going to have to bury. And
bury deep. This case was too important, and her
impartiality too crucial.

Caleb was the brother of one of her victims.
That was all he was. All he could be allowed to
be.

She went to sleep resolute. But that didn't stop
her unconscious mind from producing some
dreams that made her sleep restless and mocked
her determination to keep one dark-haired furniture maker out of the private reaches of her
mind.

Chapter 9

Emma watched as people filed into the one-room schoolhouse, pausing to sign the paper at the table set up just inside the door. Deacon Stoltzfus assured her every person who could be there would be, and promised her a list of those who were too ill or infirm to come. Since she'd already spoken to the families of the missing in depth, they'd been excused if they wished, but Emma noticed they had come anyway. Except Caleb, as yet anyway.

She saw babes in arms come in, cuddled and cooed to. She saw toddlers who would never be trusted to remain calm and silent in her world, but who were quietly obedient as they took seats on the long benches that had been moved in for this gathering.

Some of the men looked around as if they'd never been inside the building before, and she wondered how recently it had been built. It seemed solid, well constructed. Which took her mind right back to Caleb. She wrenched it away, making herself look around the room again. This time she noticed the various things on the walls: a chalkboard, shelves for books, and every few feet a poster or placard on the wall with a Bible or children's verse extolling the virtues of an obedient life. Not quite the nursery rhymes she'd grown up with. Of course, those were forever tainted in her mind. At least these were unfamiliar.

The children seemed puzzled by the change in their usual surroundings, but their parents looked mostly worried. She decided to start there. When all were seated, she walked to the front of the room. After thanking them for coming, she spoke simply and clearly.

"I know you are all worried. With good reason. I want you to know that I, the local authorities and detectives in Philadelphia are all working on this case."

She hesitated for a moment, but she'd heard enough to know they were aware of the cases in Ohio, so added, "And my colleagues in Ohio are working on that end, determining if there is indeed a link between these two horrible situations."

There was a stir in the room as a latecomer arrived. She knew who it was without even having to look. Crazy. That's what it was. How could her pulse leap without even seeing him? How could she be so sure it even was him? How would she feel if she looked to the door and saw elderly Mr. Miller instead of the man who, in a community of men who strove to be the same, still managed to stand out?

Doggedly, she went on.

"I'm here to explain that I will be contacting each of you, probably more than once, to ask you questions. Some of these questions may seem pointless to you. Some questions I may ask repeatedly. You may honestly believe you know nothing relevant, but I will be talking to you anyway. The slightest thing could matter, even if it seems unimportant to you."

In an ordinary group, questions would be peppering her by now. This group sat quietly, even the children, waiting. It was a nice change, and she tried to reward it by anticipating their questions.

"It is our recommendation that you keep girls between the ages of fifteen and twenty under close watch. The presence of adult males might be a deterrent. Don't let them walk to school alone or out to play unless in a large group."

"Our girl was not alone," someone said. "She was in a large group."

"Yes," Emma said, recognizing Miriam's distraught mother.

Although the woman didn't know it, she'd voiced Emma's biggest problem with the idea of a stranger abduction. How had he done it, three of them, out of a crowd? It seemed as if they *had* to have known him, trusted him. And that idea led to someone from within the community. Which she already knew would be met with stubborn disbelief.

"But," Emma answered, "she also didn't know there was any threat. Your girls must know there could be danger, so they can be alert, aware. That is one of their best protections."

She heard the murmuring, knew that in a community built on mutual trust, learning to distrust would go deeply against the grain. But in her view, now they had no choice.

"We have no suspects yet, nor a certain motive. We're considering every possibility we can, and please, we will entertain all theories. At this point, everything is wide open."

It seemed odd, the lack of questions from the group. She'd like to think it stemmed from faith that she knew what she was doing, but she had a feeling it was as much from the fatalistic turn of mind so many seemed to have. What will be, will be, or something.

The only thing she was sure would be was that she would be having a difficult time keeping her thoughts off that one tall, lean man in the back row.

It was all Emma could do to drive past the turnoff to the Troyer house. She'd spent the past two days talking to everyone in Paradise Ridge, many more than once.

Everybody, that is, but Caleb Troyer.

It wasn't that she'd purposely avoided him, she told herself. She was a trained professional, and she could keep even unexpected and unruly emotions in check.

What she couldn't seem to do was figure out why this man inspired them in her.

And she truly had been busy. And there were two other families hurting as Caleb was, missing their daughters, afraid for them out there in the English world they kept apart from. She supposed for them it was something like living in a peaceful village on the edge of a jungle full of predators. When one of their own vanished into that jungle of his own will it was one thing; when one of those predators came out of the jungle and attacked, it was something else entirely.

She made herself keep going past the turnoff, and halfway to the village of Paradise Ridge, she discovered it was just as well. She spotted Caleb, with Ruthie and Katie walking beside him and a sleepy-looking Grace in his arms.

No buggy? She'd seen one of the iconic Amish carriages carefully placed under cover by the side of the Troyer house.

She slowed, wondering if she should offer them a ride. Amish did ride in cars, she knew; they just wouldn't own them. It did seem rude just to drive on by. Didn't it?

She slowed even more and rolled down her passenger-side window. Ruthie, not surprisingly, spotted her first.

"Daed!" she exclaimed, giving it the Pennsylvania Dutch pronunciation as she pointed at the car. *Dad,* Emma thought, not Katie's more formal "Father." And correspondingly, Ruthie's cap was a bit askew, the loose ties hanging un-

evenly, while Katie's was precisely centered and tidily anchored.

She didn't look at the man Ruthie was speaking to. She didn't know if she was up to facing the man who had given her such a restless night first thing in the morning.

Ruthie waved. *"Guder mariye,"* she said.

"English," Katie said, and for a moment Emma thought she was describing her, before she realized the older girl was reminding her sister to speak in English for Emma's sake.

"I'm sorry," Ruthie said, flushing at this public correction.

"Good morning to you, too," Emma said, rather childishly pleased at Ruthie's relieved smile, grateful the simple greeting was one of the few phrases she remembered. Emma spoke some German thanks to a college roommate, and from childhood knew a little of the Pennsylvania Dutch the Amish routinely spoke. Probably just enough to get her into trouble, she thought wryly.

"You are off to school?" she asked.

Katie answered her with a nod. "Except for Grace. She goes to Mrs. Stoltzfus, who watches her until Ruthie or I come get her."

Emma remembered Esther Stoltzfus, a formidable woman with a stern face and an assessing look. Emma also had gotten the distinct impression, in their brief contact yesterday, that the woman had her eye on Caleb for her unmarried daughter. Emma had wondered if that was behind her offer to care for little Grace while the two older girls were at school and Caleb working in his shop. Some might think her cynical, but she was of the belief that people were people at heart, and just because the Amish perhaps had better control of ungenerous thoughts didn't mean they didn't have them.

Everybody thinks bad things now and then, Emma-girl, but that doesn't mean you act on those thoughts. That's what being a good person means.

Emma's breath caught for a moment as the memory assailed her. Her father, holding a distraught Emma, not much older than Ruthie, on his lap as he tried to explain that she wasn't evil just because she wanted to call Jackie Wasserman names back when the nasty-tempered child had started making up stories about Emma's biological parentage.

"Are you all right?"

Caleb, still holding Grace, who was a bit more awake now, was staring at Emma with interest.

"Fine," she responded, realized she sounded a bit abrupt and quickly added, "I just thought perhaps you would like a ride. I'm headed right past the school and your shop."

"May we?" Ruthie asked, sounding excited at the idea.

"It is not far," Caleb said rather stiffly.

It was true, the school was just up the road and his shop less than a mile. "That's true," Emma said neutrally. "But it is a chilly morning."

"We walk by choice," Caleb said, rubbing at his jaw. Still missing the beard, she guessed. "It is good to get the blood flowing on a cold day."

"I'm sure you're right," Emma said. She told herself not to feel stung. This man, as all Amish, lived by their own rules, and there was nothing personal in the rejection. "I was thinking of saddling up one of our horses and riding over this morning."

He lifted a brow at her, as if he'd heard something unexpected. "But you did not."

"No. I didn't want to appear as if I were…" She stopped when she realized the word she'd been about to use was *pandering.* But he seemed to understand.

"You would not. Everyone in the village knows the Coltons have lived nearby for a very long time. And that fine horses are an interest of your family." For the briefest moment she thought she saw his mouth quirk. "They might be surprised you still ride."

"They'd be more surprised if for some reason I had to chase down someone on horseback," she said.

Emma heard Ruthie giggle. The quirk almost became a smile. But it died quickly, and as quickly Emma guessed at why.

"I did not mean to make a joke about the situation or make you think I find anything amusing about any of this," she said, putting every ounce of sincerity she could muster into her voice. It wasn't hard, because it was absolutely true. And Caleb seemed to sense this, for after a moment he nodded.

"Father?" Katie's voice was quiet, somewhat tremulous, as if she dreaded interrupting her father. "We will be late for school."

"I'm sorry," Emma said quickly. "I didn't mean to make you late. Will you accept a ride now that I have?"

Caleb considered for a moment. Katie seemed very anxious, while Ruthie apparently had the wisdom to hold back the excitement that Emma had seen in her face. Riding in a car was clearly a novel and enticing experience for the lively girl.

"Very well," Caleb finally said.

With a stifled whoop of glee, Ruthie was the first to scramble into the small rear seat of the truck. Katie followed, clearly relieved that they would not be late after all. Grace was more hesitant, but both her sisters quickly soothed her and secured the seat belt Emma pointed out around her before they fastened their own, fumbling only slightly with the unfamiliar mechanisms.

And then the moment she should have realized would unsettle her—Caleb got into the front passenger seat. The cab of the ranch pickup seemed suddenly smaller. Too small.

"Is this yours, this…truck?" Ruthie asked.

"Ruthie," Caleb said, "you speak when spoken to."

Emma opened her mouth to say it was fine, then stopped, not wanting to contravene his authority. So instead she said it to him.

"I don't mind if she asks questions. That's all I did at her age."

Something changed in his eyes then; they went slightly unfocused, as if he were seeing an image in his mind. Her at Ruthie's age? Or more likely, she thought ruefully, he was picturing a Ruthie at her age, afraid she might turn out like her.

She'd heard it often yesterday. Annie, she'd been told repeatedly, had been the perfect woman: quiet, almost shy, humble and self-effacing about her considerable domestic skills.

In other words, the exact opposite of Emma herself. Although sometimes given to introspection, quiet she was not, nor shy. Humble? Well, she had four brothers, three of them older than her, so she'd certainly been humbled in her life, but humble? She didn't brag—it wasn't the Colton way—but they excelled, and that got noticed.

And of course, there was that little fact that she didn't have many domestic skills to be self-effacing about. She was a decent cook, Charlotte had seen to that, and she loved to bake, but sewing was beyond her. And as for the gas-powered wringer-style washer she'd seen in most of the Amish homes, and the vision of hanging clothes to dry during weather in the teens, the thought made her shudder. No, she likely wouldn't do well in this world.

Caleb's small nod cut off the train of thought that, surprisingly since it shouldn't have, unsettled her. It took her a moment to realize he was giving her leave to answer Ruthie's question.

"The truck belongs to the ranch," she said. "Anybody there can use it."

"You have beautiful horses there," Ruthie said.

Emma smiled. "We do. Horses were a hobby of my father's and we've been very lucky the lines have continued strong. We have three mares due this spring, and we have high hopes."

"I've seen your horses," Katie put in hesitantly. "Mother used to convince Father to go down the road along your ranch. She loved to look at them."

Caleb said nothing but something again changed. Could he not even bear the mention of his dead wife? From his own child?

"And the foals in the spring?" Emma guessed.

"Most of all," Katie said, the hesitancy wiped out by the happier memory.

"You should have come to the house, seen them up close."

"That would be too forward," Katie said gravely. "Mother wouldn't."

"We would have welcomed you." She gave the girls a glance over her shoulder. Katie looked rapt, Ruthie as if she were holding her breath and her words. "And we would now, too. Besides, now we know each other."

Katie brightened. "Yes, we do. Don't we, Father?"

Caleb made that apparently universal male sound, a cross between a grunt and "hmm," that served as a noncommittal answer to just about anything. It was so familiar to her from her own world that it made her feel absurdly warmed to hear it from him, as if their worlds weren't quite so far apart as they seemed. Some things, it appeared, never changed.

Emma chose her words carefully, keeping in mind the nature of these people. "It's good for the foals, too. They need to interact with people when they're young. So you'd actually be helping us out. In fact, perhaps this spring? If you're interested and your father is willing?"

The question was directed at Caleb, and Emma expected a repeat of the unhelpful grunt. Instead, Caleb glanced at his daughters. Emma caught a glimpse of them in the rearview mirror, two eager, innocent faces, and wondered how he could refuse them. Was he so stern he would deny them even this innocent pleasure in the outside world? She knew doing things purely for pleasure was not their way, which was why she'd brought in the idea that they would be helping with the foals, and it had the added benefit of being true.

She knew the Amish world was built on that sense of community, of all pulling for the whole, of help when needed, and she hadn't been above playing on that.

"Perhaps," Caleb finally said.

The girls squealed with delight, albeit quietly. Emma wondered if Caleb was assuming, or at least hoping, that when the time came they would have forgotten or lost interest. And maybe they would. But for now, two girls were transported at the idea of playing with baby horses, and that made her smile.

And the fact that such a simple thing had such an effect made her wonder if the simplicity of this life wasn't infecting her.

Chapter 10

It was the hands, Emma thought as she stood on the Yoder front porch, that had thrown her back to her childhood. She remembered the time when her mother had paused to chat with an Amish woman selling home-baked pies from the bakery that was down the street from the mill that was now Caleb's workshop. An impatient ten at the time, Emma had shifted restlessly, wanting to be on their way home so she could ride, while at the same time loving the luscious bakery smells.

It had been when the woman had boxed up the beautiful apple pie that Emma had noticed her hands. They were reddened and work roughened, unlike anyone's hands she'd ever seen. Her mother was no pampered flower; Charlotte Colton dug into work like any Colton. And her own hands were constantly doing, be it climbing trees, digging out horse stalls or washing the various animals that lived on the ranch, but they were still not in the shape of that woman's hands. And even in her ten-year-old brain she realized what it meant.

It meant this woman worked harder with her hands than probably all of them put together.

"It is not an easy life," her mother had explained on the way home when she'd asked. "But for them, their reward comes after this life."

At the time, Emma had thought her life rewarding enough, but now that she'd spent a few years dealing with the darker, grimmer side of adult life in her own world, she wasn't sure the Amish weren't onto something.

"—news?"

Emma snapped back to the present. She'd never been so prone to memories and introspection as she had been since she'd started this case.

It had to be being back home that had the memories stirring.

"Not yet, although Detective Colton is following a lead in Philadelphia," she said to Mrs. Yoder, who looked as concerned as she might if her own daughter were missing.

The woman nodded, her brow furrowed, as if merely the name of the huge city made her uneasy. But she invited Emma inside and offered her coffee, which at this early hour Emma accepted with genuine thanks.

As the woman busied herself with the task, Emma glanced around the room. It was, like Caleb's home, simply furnished, although she didn't see any furniture pieces on the level of Caleb's own craftsmanship. The room was bigger than Caleb's main room, but she supposed farm families ran to more children, because the more hands the better.

At that moment she heard someone on the stairs, and moments later a girl stepped into the room. At first Emma thought she was one of those children she'd been thinking about, but three things changed that assessment quickly. She was older than she had first appeared, she was wearing jeans and her blond hair was uncovered and cut short. Even an Amish girl on *rumspringa* was unlikely to cut her hair like that, even if it would accomplish what it did for this woman. Her brown eyes seemed impossibly large and expressive.

Belatedly, Emma realized there was something familiar about the woman. Even as the awareness dawned, Mrs. Yoder spoke.

"This is our guest," the woman said, but hesitated as if she wasn't sure about providing a name.

"You're from the police?" the newcomer asked, approaching. She was several inches shorter than Emma, yet there was something about her that made her seem taller. Just as, despite the soft, almost vulnerable look of her mouth, something in those doe-brown eyes warned Emma there was much more to her than that.

And not only did she look familiar, but she

sounded familiar, yet Emma was certain she'd never met her.

"FBI," Emma said, reaching for her ID in a reflexive motion. The woman stayed her with a wave of her hand. "I heard you'd come. And you look the part," she said.

Not certain exactly how that was meant, Emma wasn't sure what to say.

With a sudden smile that lit up her face and the entire room, the blonde held out a hand. "I'm Violet," she said.

Emma barely managed to keep her jaw from dropping. "Violet Chastain," she murmured.

"Yes."

Emma's mouth quirked. It wasn't that she was easily impressed by celebrity—as a Colton she'd moved in those circles before—but this one…

"No wonder you looked familiar," she said with a rueful smile at her own slowness. "There's a poster of you hanging in my kid sister's room."

And wait until I tell Piper I ran into her idol, here of all places.

Something must have shown in her face, or

else the actress was exceptionally perceptive, because she quickly explained.

"I'm researching a role," she said. "I want it to be as accurate as possible, and immersing myself in Amish life seemed the best way to achieve that." She turned to look at Mrs. Yoder with a wide smile. "And my hosts have been beyond helpful and hospitable."

"You have worked much harder than I would have expected," Mrs. Yoder said with obvious approval.

Violet turned back to Emma. "Is there any progress? Those girls—it makes my skin crawl to think what they and their families must be going through. If anything ever happened to my boys…"

Emma didn't think the shudder was put-on. In fact, for one of the hottest and most talented young stars out there, Violet Chastain seemed quite genuine.

"Were you here when the girls went missing?"

"I was, but I was in Eden Falls, where my boys are, so I didn't find out until I got back. Speaking of which, I'm off to see them now. It's been too long."

Mrs. Yoder laughed. "It was yesterday."

"Too long," Violet said with a smile that made Emma like her and her open love for her children.

The room seemed much quieter when the woman had gone, and Emma pondered a moment that larger-than-life quality, wondering if stars had it before or gained it after they became famous. But then she turned her attention back to the matter at hand and the cup of coffee Mrs. Yoder handed her. It was hot, strong and welcome.

She'd been here, on the large farm that was just down the road from Caleb's home, the first day she'd arrived. But no one had been home.

"We were attending a wedding," the woman said now when she asked. "My husband's brother. He lives near Wilkes-Barre, so we were gone three days."

Curious, she asked, "Ms. Chastain, what did she do?"

Mrs. Yoder waved a hand, much as Violet had, and Emma had the brief thought how universal some things were.

"She had meetings with movie people and stayed with her children. She is a good mother, I think."

Too bad about their father, Emma thought, but didn't say it. She doubted anyone here even knew who the tragic man who had fathered Violet Chastain's twins was.

"How well did you know the missing girls?"

"Hannah fairly well, the other two only as much as anyone else in the community."

"Was there anything that made you think Hannah might leave on her own?"

Mrs. Yoder hesitated.

"Please, Mrs. Yoder. Anything might be the one piece we need to find the girls."

"Hannah is…restless. She always has been."

"Enough to leave the faith?"

"Perhaps." The woman sighed, looking troubled. "Of all the children of age, Hannah leaving would surprise me the least."

Emma appreciated the woman's honesty. Or perhaps it was simply that living, in essence, next door, she was more aware. Although it seemed that the striking redhead had a temperament to match her hair, and Emma wondered how someone like that would fit into this quiet community.

Or someone like herself.

Emma gave herself an inward shake, annoyed at the way her thoughts kept slipping away from her. She must be truly going sour on the world if all she could do was contrast the cruelty man could visit upon his fellow man that she dealt with on a regular basis, with the way these people all looked out for each other.

Not that there wasn't much to be admired, of course. And at that word, something else popped into her head.

"Did Hannah get along with her brother?"

"With Caleb? Of course. Caleb's a very amiable man."

Emma barely kept her brows from arching upward. She'd found him gruff, at best. Was he really that different to his own people? Was it only outsiders who got treated to that aspect of him? And all outsiders? Or just her?

She found herself hoping it was all. She didn't want to think it was she alone who set him on edge.

Then again… Even as she thought it, a rush of warmth started somewhere in her middle and shot upward. It had been a long time since she'd felt such a response. That she was feeling it now, to a man who was…impossible, seemed just another irony in her life.

She didn't think anything showed in her face, but Mrs. Yoder said, "Caleb will have to remarry soon. He has his girls to think of. They need a mother."

"They had a mother," Emma said, telling herself that the tiny bit of sharpness that had crept into her voice stemmed from empathy for the girls who had lost their mother, not embarrassment that this woman might have read her feelings.

Or worse, that she herself didn't like the idea of Caleb remarrying.

"Yes, and Annie was a fine, fine woman. Kind, loving, generous, properly humble, she led a good life, and I'm certain her reward was great."

There was unshakable faith in her voice, and Emma couldn't help contrasting the quiet acceptance of death with the way the outside world handled it. Or didn't handle it, in too many cases.

"Caleb loved her very much. They picked each other out when they were just Katie's age, and they never wavered. We all knew they were destined to be together."

"They married young, then?"

"They were nineteen, I believe."

Emma couldn't help doing the math. Caleb was thirty-one, the file had said. So he had been with his Annie for seventeen years, married for nine. That kind of longevity for someone who was only thirty-one was rare in her world, and again she had that thought that these people were onto something.

"That's…remarkable," Emma said.

"Annie was a quiet sort, almost shy. But she had a way about her. All those girls who are thinking they'll step into her shoes will find them harder to fill than they might think."

Don't, Emma told herself. *Don't pursue this. It has nothing to do with your investigation.*

"I'm sure they're lined up for miles," she said, a little surprised at how fierce her voice sounded. But quiet and shy was not something she did well, and if that was Caleb's ideal…

If Mrs. Yoder noticed the sudden sharpness, she didn't let on. "Of course. Caleb is a handsome man, and he makes a good living. And in his way he is as quietly generous as Annie was. He's always the first one there when someone needs help."

"Admirable," she said, although the meaning now was entirely different than when she'd thought it before.

"Yes. But he's clearly in no hurry. So the hopefuls continue to swoon and giggle."

The description nearly made Emma laugh, and

that gave her the edge she'd needed to get control and steer the conversation back to the matter at hand. It also put her back in control of her emotions. "Swoon and giggle" was hardly in her repertoire. No matter how much Caleb Troyer might make her weak at the knees with his misty-gray eyes and his strong hands.

She'd be better off falling for a suspect, she told herself sternly. It would be less impossible.

And then she was back at sea again, not liking the acknowledgment she'd just made that she could be falling for Caleb Troyer.

Chapter 11

He could not, Caleb thought, say the FBI agent wasn't doing her job. The woman had been everywhere, talked to everyone. And if she'd learned anything useful, she wasn't saying.

Or at least, she wasn't saying it to him.

He should be glad of that, he told himself. Her brisk, no-nonsense manner grated on him. He preferred quiet, gentle women like his wife had been.

And why he was even comparing the two was beyond him.

He paced the length of the shop, glancing at the clock, then frowning as he remembered he'd forgotten to wind it yesterday and it must have stopped sometime this afternoon. Just another sign of his lack of focus.

For all the work he was getting done, he might as well just close up and go get Katie and Ruthie from school, then go retrieve Grace from Mrs. Stoltzfus. He'd put down the heavy wood plane once he'd realized he was so distracted he'd likely lose a finger if he continued. Distracted by an overwhelming worry about Hannah. By wondering how he would ever tell the girls if the worst were to happen.

By the woman who was here to find that out.

His jaw tightened as he clamped down on unwelcome thoughts. Again. He was just impatient, hard though he tried to rein in the desperate urge to do…something. Anything. That was all it was.

He remembered something his father had always hammered into him as a boy: whenever you felt you had the least control was when you needed control the most. Caleb had never been able to picture his stern, stoic father out of control, so he guessed he was quoting someone else.

Perhaps his own father, Caleb's grandfather, who had been a bit of a wild one by all accounts, chafing at the restrictions of his life until one day he'd fallen just as wildly in love and everything had changed for him.

Odd, Caleb thought. He hadn't realized until now that his grandmother, the woman who had brought that wild heart to heel, bore a certain resemblance to Emma Colton.

He turned and paced back toward the front of the shop. The piece he was working on was a commissioned job, a large cabinet for a wealthy client in nearby York. It wouldn't do to give it any less than his full attention. He simply must get control of his rampaging thoughts. He'd never had trouble focusing on his work before. In fact, after Annie's death it had been his salvation, and he'd poured his grief into long hours of work.

That it didn't seem to be working now frustrated him. He didn't understand why it was failing him, what was different—

He stopped midstride, his breath catching in

his throat. The vision before him tightened his chest so that he could barely breathe. For there were his two oldest girls, walking to the shop as they often did when school let out. Only they weren't alone. Emma Colton was with them. She was more than with them.

She was between them, a girl clinging to each hand with a trust he found a little stunning considering she was not just a stranger but an outsider, as well. Katie was walking with her head slightly down, as she often did, but Ruthie was looking up into Emma's face, clearly involved in a conversation that had her fascinated.

And Emma showed no sign of unease, awkwardness or desire to escape. In fact, as he stood there staring, she leaned down and said something to Katie that made the girl smile and apparently join in the conversation.

And all the while Emma held those two trusting little hands securely, almost protectively.

Caleb swallowed tightly. He turned his head, unable to look at the pleasant, unexpected tableau any longer. And unable to deal with the unwelcome feelings it stirred in him.

Be honest at least, he told himself. *God knows your thoughts.*

It wasn't the idyllic picture of his daughters strolling hand in hand with a lovely woman that had made his gut clench. It was Emma herself, the late-fall sunlight turning her hair into that rich fire he wanted to warm himself in.

"You are done with that," he said aloud, as if only vocalizing the words could make it so. "Annie is gone, and with her your heart. That part of your life is over."

He could hear, echoing in his head, all the protestations of the community, telling him thirty-one was far too young for him to give up and that his girls needed a mother.

He'd thought about that long and hard. He was fortunate in that his work brought him enough income to pay to have done the things he could not do, things that Annie had always done. And out of need, he'd learned to be an adequate cook, although Katie, even at eleven, was going to outstrip him in that realm soon. She'd already taken over breakfast and preparing her own and her sisters' lunches for school, leaving only dinner to him.

"Ah, Annie," he said quietly into the air, thinking of all the years he'd come home from work to find a hot, hearty meal waiting, "I didn't appreciate you enough."

And then he heard the girls' chatter as they opened the door to the shop. Lighthearted, eager, happy. It was like a saw blade slicing through him to realize how long it had been since he'd heard his girls sound like that.

Perhaps they did need a mother.

But certainly an Englishwoman, and an FBI agent of all things, was not an acceptable choice.

"Hello," Emma said with a hesitant smile as she closed the shop door behind her. "I hope you don't mind. I saw the girls walking this way and joined them."

Caleb shook his head. With a last, stern command to himself to betray nothing of his undesirable thoughts, he made himself speak evenly.

"I do not mind. The...protection is welcome."

Emma studied him for a moment. "I don't think you need to worry," she finally said.

Not worry? Caleb couldn't believe she'd said that. How could he not worry?

"Agent Emma said—"

"What did you call her?" Caleb asked, cutting Ruthie's burst of excitement short. Katie colored fiercely and backed up a step.

"We compromised," Emma said, so quickly Caleb wondered if she was explaining so the girls wouldn't have to. "I wanted them to call me Emma, but Mrs. Stoltzfus pointed out that was improper for girls their age."

"I'm sure she did," Caleb said before he could stop himself. Esther Stoltzfus had long ago appointed herself arbiter of decorum and social niceties, and he himself had more than once run afoul of her dictates.

He sent the girls off to the office in the back of the shop to begin their homework. And before he said something he didn't want them to hear.

He seemed to have far too much trouble controlling his words when "Agent Emma" was around.

"Does she always correct visitors?" Emma asked.

"She corrects everyone," Caleb said. He could hear Annie's gentle voice chiding him and added hastily, "But she means well."

"Sometimes," Emma said, "good intentions don't matter. Results do. Katie was very embarrassed."

Something had come into the woman's voice, something fierce, and it took Caleb a moment to realize she was feeling defensive. Of Katie. That knowledge rattled him even more than the lovely picture of her walking toward him holding hands with his girls had.

"Katie must toughen up," he said, his unease with his continuingly inappropriate reaction to this woman making his voice more gruff than he had intended.

"She will," Emma said flatly. "Life will do that to her soon enough. No need to rush it."

Caleb let out a breath he hadn't even been

aware of holding. How often had he said just that to others who had commented on Katie's sensitivity? She was so like her mother in that respect that when others said what he'd reactively said about her toughening up, he took it as a criticism of Annie, and that he would not accept gracefully.

Yet here was this woman who had dropped into their lives just three days ago understanding and defending Katie in the same way he often had.

"Do you…have children?" he asked, wondering why the idea unsettled him, yet thinking it must be the answer to her easy empathy and connection with the girls.

"No," she said. "But I've been around them a lot. My parents ran a foundation for at-risk kids, and all of us were deeply involved."

Caleb shook his head slowly. "'At-risk kids.' What kind of world is it where such a term can even exist?"

"A cruel one," Emma said with a grimace. "No

wonder you set yourselves apart. Your lives are much…cleaner."

Caleb heard the tinge of bitterness in her voice. He knew enough of the English world to deal with it as he had to, and he rarely dwelt upon it more than that. But he knew of the Coltons from knowing Dr. Colton, knew they were wealthy and exceedingly generous, with their hearts as well as their wealth. If their world could bring such a feeling even to someone like Emma Colton…

"I thought of leaving, once."

Emma gave him a startled look. "Leaving… Paradise Ridge? Or your faith?"

"Both. After my wife died, all I wished was to leave, get away, escape."

He stopped, stunned that he had said it, that he had told this stranger, this woman, this English, what he had told no one else. Ever.

"I've found," Emma said, her voice now quiet, gentle and full of empathy, burning out the bitter note, "that it's never a good or successful idea to run away from something. To run *to* something, yes. But away? It will only follow you."

He wondered what had taught her that hard lesson. Something awful; he could see the haunted shadow of it in her eyes.

"Or you will carry it with you," he said, "and end where you began."

"Exactly that," she said. "Wise of you. Most people have to do it to learn it."

He gave a half shrug. "I could not do it. After losing their mother, I could not take my daughters away from the only life they'd ever known, the community they are part of, the other people who care for them."

"Including your sister?"

"Especially my sister," Caleb said. He shook his head, feeling a stab of guilt. "I should not be dwelling on my small difficulties when she is in jeopardy."

"You can't worry every minute," Emma said, reminding Caleb of what she'd said earlier.

"What did you mean when you said I didn't have to worry?"

"I meant that this predator seems to have a type, and your girls don't match that type."

"But my sister did?"

Hannah nodded. Then, hastily, as if to forestall any further questions about that particular question, she went on.

"I wanted to let you know I've turned up a couple of possible leads. Someone mentioned seeing a UPS truck in the area that day, so we're tracking down the driver to see if he saw anything unusual. And I'll be on my way to check with the police department in Harrisburg. They stopped an older man driving a van with a couple of young girls in it."

Caleb drew back sharply. "Hannah?"

"No, sorry," Emma said quickly. "They sent me photos, and neither girl is a match to any of ours. It may well be nothing, just coincidence, but I don't want to miss anything that could possibly be related."

Any of ours.

She'd said it as if she truly felt it. As if the missing girls were a part of her own community.

He liked that despite the touch of bitterness he'd seen before, she could still feel that way.

There were depths to Agent Emma Colton that were intriguing.

He recoiled. That way of thinking led to nothing but trouble. Lovely, empathetic and smart, she was all of that. And yes, intriguing.

And to him, apparently, dangerous.

Chapter 12

There was no doubt about it, Emma thought as she drove back from Harrisburg in the rapidly fading light after chasing the lead that had indeed been unrelated. The older man had simply been transporting his niece and her best friend back home after a weekend at his farm. An afternoon wasted, yet necessarily.

No, no doubt at all—every woman she'd met in Paradise Ridge had her sights on Caleb, either for herself or her daughter or niece or a friend.

She could understand why, of course. All the practical reasons: he made a good living, had a solidly built home, a nice buggy and, from the brief glance she'd gotten when the girls had pointed him out, a strong, steady sorrel gelding to pull it.

As for the impractical reasons, he had those in spades, too. That tall, strong body, the light color of his eyes against dark hair, the strong, even features. And his hands. Those talented, dexterous, strong yet gentle hands that created such beauty. She could go into raptures over those hands.

Lord, she *was* going into raptures over them.

As a distraction, she tried to picture him with the mustache-less beard Amish tradition demanded of married men, a look so foreign to her world. But no matter what she did, she couldn't make him anything less than the most handsome man she'd seen in a very long time.

Her fingers drummed against the steering wheel, not idly like someone stuck in traffic, but with purpose. What purpose she wasn't sure, unless it was to dissipate some of the excess energy and emotion that seemed to pile up in her every time her mind turned to Caleb Troyer.

When she realized, as she approached Paradise Ridge, that her subconscious mind had assumed she was headed for Caleb's house, she took her foot off the accelerator and nearly hit the brakes. Reflexively she looked in the rearview mirror, as if she had to know what kind of chaos she would have caused had she done so.

None, it seemed. There wasn't a car to be seen behind her. The tourist season was winding down, she supposed. The last of the autumn leaves had vanished, and the weather was turning from brisk to downright cold. No snow yet, but the inevitability of it hovered. And this time of year the days ended early, with sunset before five o'clock.

A tiny sigh escaped her as she thought of the Double C in winter, blanketed in pristine white, one of her favorite times of year. Building snow creatures—she'd always had a knack for particularly lifelike dogs—snow forts and the usual snowball fights with her brothers. It had usually ended up Derek and Tate against her and Gunnar, who, with oldest-brother instincts and that

Colton sense of responsibility, had always sided with her in those epic battles.

And now Gunnar was fighting an epic battle of his own, with his own mind and memories.

She fought down her chronic worry; they all knew there was nothing they could do to help their big brother until he admitted he needed it.

She'd managed to distract herself, finally, but the end result was that she'd ended up at Caleb's house as if the car had been on autopilot. It wasn't that she didn't have reason to be here. If he was a man of her world, she could simply have called him with the information that the lead in Harrisburg had gone nowhere. But he was not, and the only way she had to tell him was face-to-face.

Part of her cringed inwardly at the idea of living without even a telephone except the one used for emergencies. It sat in an outside booth—to discourage any long, cozy winter chats, she supposed—beside Deacon Stoltzfus's home. A second was in the small commercial district, outside the bakery. And that was the extent of the wired connection with the outside world.

She knew the reasons, knew that it was all part of the protection of the community. When you didn't have a phone, you had to maintain in-person connections with the people in your life, which in turn fostered the sense of community the Amish world rested upon. Cell phones, she knew, were still a topic of much debate in the varied Amish communities, their unwired nature making them acceptable for some, while others felt the same principles applied.

And yet, while the modern, connected part of her cringed, another part of her yearned for the peace that would come if she simply dumped her smartphone. She'd shut it off for a long period after her personal visit to hell two years ago, and it had been…restorative, if unsettling to her friends and family.

The house was more prepared for cars than many Amish homes, probably because of what Caleb had told her about his father using the beautifully built place as an advertisement for his skills. Pride, she knew, was a particular sin for these people, but satisfaction in work well done was something else.

For a moment after she turned off the engine, she just sat there, looking at the house. At the glow of the lamps through the windows, seeming somehow warmer and more golden than electric lighting. She guessed there was likely a fire going in the woodstove, the girls were probably finishing their homework at the solid, simple table built by their father, and it suddenly seemed so appealing she wished she could simply step inside and belong.

Shaken by the fierceness of that wish, she nearly started the car and drove away. She was, in fact, reaching for the key in the ignition when the front door of the house opened. Caleb stood there, no doubt having heard the unaccustomed sound of the engine.

"Well, now you're stuck," she muttered and instead pulled the keys out and put them in her jacket pocket. She slipped reluctantly out of the car.

"Agent Em—Colton?"

There was no excuse for the silly leap her heart took as she heard him make the abrupt shift from the name the girls called her to the more formal Agent Colton. But the leap was followed by a tumble, as she wondered why he'd begun to use the girls' term. Had she been a topic of conversation? Had he perhaps warned them not to get too close to the outsider? Or fond of her? It would be typical, she thought as she closed the distance between them.

And it would hurt, she admitted. Because she had already become fond of those girls. Katie, with her shy sensitivity, Ruthie, all live wire and bristling intelligence, and sweet little Grace. They had an innocence she couldn't help but respond to, and that innocence fired even further her determination that this ugliness not mar their lives forever.

Not to mention that the thought of what their beloved Hannah and her friends could be going through sent dual knives of horror and fury through her.

"Are you all right?"

His voice had changed, warmed, taken on a note of concern. She could only imagine what her face must have looked like.

"I'm…fine." It took her a moment to get out the lie. Great time for that endless loop of unforgettable images to start running in her mind, she thought, with the strongest sense of bitterness she'd felt in months. She marshaled her energy, knowing what it would take to beat the images back and maintain control.

"You do not look fine," he said bluntly. "Come inside and sit down."

He was an amazing combination of strength and gentleness, a combination too often lacking in the men of her world. Outside her brothers, that is. It was undeniably compelling, and she followed him inside.

The girls were indeed at the table, books and papers spread before them. They greeted her happily, but at a single word from Caleb went back to their schoolwork.

Little Grace was in a tiny wood rocking

chair—no doubt built by her father's loving hands—in front of the woodstove, looking at her with wide-eyed curiosity. She'd not seen that much of the toddler, only enough to see what a beautiful child she was, chubby-cheeked, with the nearly white-blond curls of childhood.

And he was a man in the difficult position of single father, yet while stern, he never seemed to lose his gentleness with his girls. And they clearly adored him, which told her much; she'd seen too many kids who feared or downright hated their parents not to see the difference.

And even though he had the help of his community, a strong, united sort of help you would also rarely find in her world, he was raising them himself. And in his way, helping the community as much as anyone. The deacon, a rule-enforcing sort of man, had unbent long enough to reiterate what Mrs. Yoder had told her, that when someone in the community needed financial help, or there was a barn to be built, or repairs to be done, Caleb was the first in line.

Yes, he was a man who would be considered admirable in either world....

After my wife died, all I wished was to leave, get away, escape....

She remembered now his stunned look in the moment after he'd spoken those words. She realized now he hadn't meant to let that out, about having wanted to leave.

He led her to the same chair she'd sat in before. She took it gratefully, although she shouldn't feel so weak when she'd done more driving today than anything else. But she knew the real reason, knew how much fighting that tide of memories took out of her, and this was the strongest fight she'd had to put up in some time.

Moments later he was back, holding out a cup of coffee to her. "There is sugar and milk, if you wish."

"No, thank you, this is perfect," she said as she took the cup and cradled it in hands that welcomed the warmth. The deep, rich liquid gave her a jolt that was as welcome as the warmth, and she felt a bit more in control.

"There is bad news," he said, and it wasn't a question. All movement from the table stopped, and Ruthie and Katie both turned their heads.

It took her mind, still divided by the effort to shove vicious memories back in their cage, a moment to process that he had, quiet naturally, assumed that her tension was due to bearing bad news.

"No, no," she said hastily. "I'm sorry, I didn't mean to give you that impression. There's no news."

She explained what she'd found in Harrisburg. She saw him let out a long breath.

"Sometimes no news is good news," she said.

"For how long?" he asked.

She realized what he was asking, how long before not knowing became worse than knowing the truth, even if the truth was the worst.

"We'll find them," she said, her jaw tightening.

The images rose again, battling against all her efforts, trying to find a way around all the techniques she'd ever been taught about how to keep them at bay. She had no way of knowing if what they were going through was anything like what she'd endured two years ago, but she couldn't seem to stop imagining Hannah and her friends in a similar dark, evil place.

"Girls? Mind your schoolwork. We will be in the kitchen."

We will? Emma thought, puzzled and, thankfully, distracted.

But she followed, thinking perhaps there was something he wished to ask her out of earshot of the girls. The kitchen was barely that, being just around a corner but not really a separate room.

He pulled out a chair at a table that was a twin to the one out front, except for being made of a different kind of wood, with a redder tone and the most amazing pattern of grain she'd seen since…since she'd seen the sideboard in his shopwindow.

She sat down, unable to stop herself from reaching out to trace the pattern with a fingertip.

"You are truly an artist, Caleb." She realized instantly she'd used his first name, hardly proper protocol. "I'm sorry. Mr. Troyer."

He looked at her for a long moment, then took the chair to her right. "Caleb will do."

She let out a breath of relief that he hadn't taken offense.

"Emma, then. Please."

After a moment's hesitation, he nodded. She took a long sip of the coffee, needing the restorative jolt.

"What is it," he asked, "that you're not saying?"

She knew then that the horror of that parade of memories had shown in her face.

Or Caleb Troyer was more perceptive than she'd given him credit for.

"It's nothing to do with Hannah."

"What is it, then, that made you look terrified and furious at the same time?"

Okay, more perceptive wins, she thought. With an effort, she said merely, "I loathe predators who target women and children."

"They are among the most loathsome of creations," Caleb said evenly, not as if he didn't believe it, but as if he believed it so profoundly it didn't require any emphasis. And after a moment of studying her, he said quietly, "You have seen much of such things."

The memories assailed her, and she couldn't stop the bitter sounding "Too much" from escaping. "It is why I must always fight the urge to be judge, jury and executioner when it comes to that particular sort of predator."

"That you are able to is a testament to your strength," he said quietly.

She was startled at how deeply the quiet compliment touched her. Uncertain how to respond—was she ever *not* uncertain around this man?—she murmured, "Sometimes I don't feel very strong."

"And yet you continue. Strength doesn't mean you smash all opposition. It means you simply keep going in the face of it."

She stared at him, at this man who lived a life so different from her own, plain, simple, free of the technology and chaos that her own world seemed to rain down upon them all.

Such words from such a quarter reminded her that wisdom didn't always descend from more hallowed halls than a simple Amish house.

Chapter 13

"Believe me, I'd help if I could. But out there, I'm too busy just trying to find my way around to notice much. They need more street signs out there."

"I suppose they all know where they're going," Emma said to the young delivery driver who, while more than cooperative, apparently hadn't seen—or hadn't noticed—anything helpful.

"If we come up with anything specific to ask you about, I may be back."

The young man looked her up and down unabashedly. "Anytime," he said with a grin.

The compliment was obvious, and Emma appreciated it. But Caleb's quiet comment on her strength last night had meant much more to her. Because it wasn't a reaction to her looks? Or because it had come from him?

She wasn't sure. And she wasn't sure she wanted to know.

The driver worked a later shift, so the sun was fading as she headed back to Paradise Ridge. She had to pass the spot where the missing girls had last been seen. Although she'd already spent several hours there over the past few days, she stopped again.

For a moment she just stood there, looking at the big, red barn. She had seen an Amish barn raising as a child; her father had taken her to watch. And she'd noticed, even then, that he'd been as intrigued as she had been.

"Teamwork," he'd murmured. "The living, breathing example of perfect teamwork."

She walked around, her eyes always searching. It was unlikely but always possible some clue had been missed. She focused on the ground around the barn first, including the three stepped-back stone retaining walls. These, too, had obviously been built by a superior craftsman; the intricate placing of stones without mortar was as much of an art form as the barn itself.

This was a larger barn than the one she'd seen built that day long ago. And it had taken longer than the single day that one had. It looked as new as it was, as yet unweathered, its fresh red paint clean and almost shiny. No one would ever guess that shortly after its completion, this quiet community would be thrown into chaos.

It was as she was rounding the large feed silo attached to the side of the barn that she heard a noise from inside. She frowned slightly; the local deputies had asked the family who owned the barn to keep it clear until the lab had finished processing the huge inventory of evidence that had been gathered. Witnesses had reported each of the three girls being seen in various locations at the party just before they went missing, and each of those locations had had to be searched, any possible evidence gathered, cataloged and processed.

That the delay in calling the authorities might

have made all that work a moot point was something she tried not to dwell upon.

She walked around to the far end of the barn where there was a small door next to the larger, sliding doors. It was open.

She wasn't really concerned, but she did check her sidearm, clearing her jacket out of the way and resting her right hand on the grip. She closed her eyes for a moment, both to enhance her listening and to start the adjustment of her vision to what would be a darker interior. Then she stepped inside, taking care to make no sound.

She spotted him immediately, the man who stood near the center of the big space. Her breath caught, her pulse sped up. His back was to her, and his clothes were indistinguishable from any other man's in the community. But she knew. Somehow, she knew.

As if he'd sensed her presence, he went very still. And slowly, he turned around.

For a moment, she couldn't move. And he didn't move. Yet she felt a pull, unlike anything she'd ever felt before, as if some invisible, unbreakable wire connected them. And it was being reeled in, creating that pull.

In almost the same instant they both moved. Slowly at first, as if he was resisting as much as she. As if he were as reluctant as she. As if he felt the same sense of fighting the inevitable that she was feeling.

She tried to laugh at herself and her unaccustomed sense of drama. This wasn't some big, dramatic moment, filled with atmosphere and tension.

Unless you make it one, she thought with a wry quirk of her mouth.

He had a perfectly good reason to be here. A couple, in fact. Not only was this where his sister had been last seen alive and well, he'd been one of the lead builders on this project. This was a position, she'd been told, that was usually held by older members of the community, with more experience, but no one had more skill as a carpenter than Caleb Troyer.

But he hadn't been working. He'd been simply

standing, his head tilted back, as if studying the huge rafters.

Or looking for answers, she thought as she came to a halt, again at the same moment he did, when they were a bare couple of feet apart.

She suddenly felt as if they were totally alone in the world. The barn felt even more hollow and cavernous than it was. He was watching her, steadily, not in a leering way, but as if she were a piece of lumber and he had to assess her value and use for his work. It was a bit unsettling, and she grimaced inwardly at her own inconsistency. Wasn't she always focused on making people judge her by her work, her usefulness, and not her gender and looks? And now here was a man who seemed to be doing just that, and she was reacting like...

She wasn't sure what she was reacting like. She had no basis for comparison. Nothing in her experience to liken it to, because no one had ever caused this kind of reaction in her. It took every bit of determination she had in her to hold his gaze, to not look away hastily, like some infatuated child caught staring at the object of her adoration.

Something in his gaze changed, shifted; even in the dimmer light inside the barn she could see it.

"Emma."

He'd said her name before, since they'd agreed to the first-name basis, but not like this. Never like this, as if he'd fought every letter of it, as if he'd lost the battle not to say it at all.

As if he were as tangled up as she seemed to be, every time she was around him.

"Caleb," she said. But for her it was a battle to make herself say it, to get the name out in anything close to a normal voice.

She didn't succeed very well. In her own ears, all she could hear was an open note of husky longing, and she wished she'd not said it at all. For the sound of her own voice seemed to make real, to acknowledge, the attraction she'd been fighting since the first moment she'd laid eyes on this man.

His right hand lifted, toward her face. She held

her breath, not daring to move. For the barest instant, his fingers brushed over her cheek.

He yanked his hand back as if she'd burned him. He stared at the fingertips that had touched her skin, as if they no longer belonged to him. His expression was one of such shock she couldn't help but wonder if he truly hadn't been aware of what he'd been doing.

Or if perhaps his fingers were simply burning, as was the cheek he'd touched.

"It's a beautiful barn," she said, wondering as soon as the words were out if she could have picked anything more inane to say.

For a long moment he just stared at her. Emma had the unsettling feeling he could hear her heart pounding, that it was echoing in the cavernous space. And she wished that she'd left it to him to speak first, just to see what he would have said after that brief but electrifying touch.

"It will stand."

And that, she thought, was the quintessential Amish compliment. The beauty of something was never the goal; the functionality and sturdiness was what mattered.

"Your furniture is beautiful."

He blinked at the seeming non sequitur. Then, slowly, almost warily, he nodded.

"You can admit that, but not that this barn is?"

She was genuinely puzzled and spoke that way.

His expression cleared. "My work must appeal to outsiders."

She considered that. Then nodded. "Okay. I get that." She glanced around at the huge space. "Then it's a very…large barn."

For a moment she thought he was going to smile. "A fact," he said.

"And red," she added, barely able to stop from smiling herself. Was she imagining that he was still fighting an answering smile?

"Another fact."

"And therefore acceptable."

"I believe you have it now."

The smile broke through then. A smile that made her grin back at him in a kind of delight she hadn't felt in far too long.

And then he laughed.

It was short, barely more than a chuckle, but real and all the more precious because he'd fought it. And the sound sent her pulse racing as quickly as that brief brush of his fingers had, a fact that rattled her.

She doubted he'd laughed since Hannah and her friends had disappeared. She wondered if he'd laughed since his wife had died.

Unfortunately—or perhaps not—the moment didn't last.

"Why are you here again?" he asked.

"When in doubt, go back to the scene," she said.

"Doubt?"

She sighed. "The delivery driver was no help. He might be, eventually, if we turn up something specific to ask him about, but nobody seems to have seen anything out of the ordinary that day."

Caleb glanced around at the barn. "Hannah was here, the day we built it. She made her pies the day before, so that she could watch. She always liked to see how the pieces came together," he said. "She said it was like sewing a dress—none of the pieces make sense until they start to come together."

Emma smiled. And then, softly, determinedly, she said, "I can't wait to meet her."

He went very still. Then he turned to her, understanding and thanks in his eyes as acknowledgment of her careful, resolute phrasing.

"You will like her, I think." His own words were an acceptance of hers. "And she will like you." He rubbed a hand over his jaw, and she wondered if the habit was a subconscious awareness of the missing beard. "Too much, perhaps."

Emma winced. But then she reined in her reaction born of emotions she shouldn't be allowing anyway. She made herself think, then ask quietly, without hurt or rancor, "Too much?"

"We always worried about Hannah. She is a restless spirit, and it is those we most often lose to…the outside."

"To my world," she said, guessing that was what he'd originally intended to say.

"Yes," he had the grace to admit.

"And yet," she said, the investigator coming to the fore now, "you insist she hasn't just gone to join that world."

He immediately picked up on the change in her. "I do not say that she would not, in the end, leave us. What I do say, what I know to my bones, is that she would not do it this way, without a word, simply disappearing without even a goodbye."

Which means she didn't leave of her own volition, Emma thought. But she didn't say it, knew Caleb knew perfectly well what the subtext was here.

"Especially to the girls," he added, and for the first time pain echoed in his voice. "She adores them."

So his own emotions were kept strictly in check. But cause pain to his children, and he was not so stoic. That told her a lot about him, she thought.

"Where are the girls?"

"Grace is still with Mrs. Stoltzfus. Katie and Ruthie are at a youth group gathering at the Yoders'." He glanced toward one of the barn windows that faced west, seemed to realize the time. "I must go. They will be home soon."

"It's getting dark quickly," she said. "May I give you a ride home? I have to go past your place anyway. And we can stop for Grace on the way."

He hesitated, but another glance at the sharply slanted light coming through the window seemed to decide him. "I would be thankful," he said.

"Just don't offer to pay me like Esther Stoltzfus did, please. Let a person do a favor."

He seemed startled, and she wondered if perhaps he had been going to do just that, offer to pay her as if she were one of the many locals who served as a sort of Amish taxi service.

"I was only going to invite you to join us for dinner," he said.

She blinked. "You were?"

"Katie is preparing the meal this evening. Her meat loaf. She would be honored to have a guest share it."

"I... Thank you. I would enjoy that."

She saw something flash in his eyes, something that looked akin to what she was feeling. Which was silly, given that what she was feeling was such a tangled mess of anticipation, excitement and wishing she hadn't agreed that she couldn't begin to sort them out.

Chapter 14

Emma should have felt much guiltier about this. Socializing with adjuncts to an investigation wasn't exactly forbidden, especially if it could forward the investigation, but it was likely to be looked at intently.

And somehow she doubted playing a surprisingly raucous form of Scrabble—something the girls called "speed Scrabble"—would ever be considered as furthering the investigation.

But at the moment, she didn't care. Once she'd accepted the invitation, she decided to shed her misgivings, for Katie's sake if nothing else. And Caleb had apparently decided to at least conceal his, as well. As a result the meal, after a solemn prayer, had been lively with chatter, the girls as interested in her life as she was in theirs.

Caleb seemed mostly to listen and watch the three females with an almost bemused expression. Grace had also watched, wide-eyed, in a special, taller chair that let her sit at the table with them. Emma couldn't help noticing how gentle Caleb was with the toddler, tidying up as the excited child would inadvertently knock something over or drop food or a utensil.

Many men would have taken their grief and anger out on the child who had cost her mother her life. Would have resented her for being here when his beloved wife was gone. Or perhaps that was only men in her world. Here it would likely be seen as the will of God and accepted, however cruel it might seem.

Over the meal Katie explained in great detail how she had prepared the food without many of the modern conveniences Emma was used to. Ruthie, who apparently was not a fan of kitchen work, still had to pipe in now and then with the little bits she'd done to help.

After the meal, Emma had insisted on helping Katie clean up, and the three females had quickly worked out an efficient system of washing, drying, putting away and dodging Grace's efforts to help. Finally Caleb bade the little girl say good-night and took her to bed, over a quiet protest that would have been a howl in her world.

And then Ruthie had suggested the fast-paced version of the familiar game.

"I should warn you," Caleb had said mildly, "she's quite the expert."

"A Scrabble shark, is she?"

"A what?" Ruthie asked.

"A card shark is what you call someone who lures innocent bystanders into a card came by pretending ignorance of the game and then proceeds to trounce them soundly."

Ruthie giggled.

"Is that dishonest?" Katie asked solemnly.

"I suppose that depends on who you ask," Emma said, with a glance at Caleb. She was treading on parental ground here. "Some would say it's the mark—that's the person who gets tricked—that it's his own fault because he should have known better. Others would say the card shark was dishonest, yes."

"What would you say?" Ruthie demanded.

Again she glanced at Caleb and had the strangest feeling he was waiting to see what she would say as much as the girls.

"If it was a game for fun, it's a lesson learned. If it was for money, then I'd be looking at it a lot closer."

The girls seemed to accept that, and the game had begun. Once it had, there was little time for discussion. This wasn't called speed Scrabble for nothing.

Ruthie was indeed a shark. She might not always go for the longest words, but she was quick and kept them all hopping. Although Caleb twice called a challenge on words that seemed to have sprung from Ruthie's fertile imagination. Once she had gone to the big dictionary on the bookshelf and seemed surprised not to find her word there. The second time, she merely grinned and shrugged, conceding the challenge.

So there was no coddling here, no allowing the child to win under false pretenses, Emma thought as the game pieces were finally picked up and carefully stored away. She liked that. Being prepared for reality was one of the best ways to deal with it, her father had always said.

She felt an old pang she'd not felt in a while, remembering similar nights with her parents, nights spent playing games or just having round-house family discussions that sometimes became a free-for-all of teasing, pillow-tossing, but over-flowing with the kind of love she could easily have never known had Donovan and Charlotte Colton not been the people they were.

"You seem sad," Caleb said after he'd sent the older girls off to prepare for bed.

Emma didn't dissemble. "Just nostalgic. And missing my folks."

Caleb smiled and gave a slow, thoughtful nod. "It is good that you don't forget them."

"I could never forget them. They were the most remarkable people I've ever known. If not for them, who knows where all six of us would have ended up."

"You were all adopted?"

Emma nodded and gave him the brief history of the Colton tradition of building families with kids who had nowhere else to go. She also told him about Butterfly Hearts, the organization her parents had built to help inner-city kids, because "they couldn't adopt everybody."

"They sound like remarkable people."

"They were." She made no effort to conceal the love that rang in her voice. "And my siblings and I are determined to make sure their legacy continues."

"Admirable."

He sounded so sincere she gave him a quizzical look. "So there are things in the outside world you...approve of?"

His mouth quirked. "I am not the judge of such things. But I do believe the ways of that world are what makes things like your parents' work necessary."

She grimaced. "I can't argue with that."

"And," he added, almost musingly, as if he were thinking out loud, "in your own way, in your work, I suppose you try to deal with those negative ways, to limit them, or their effects."

"That's exactly how I look at it."

She was beyond startled. Once again she had underestimated his perceptiveness. Was she so blinded by the fact that he was Amish that she had expected not only ignorance of her world, but that he'd never even thought about it?

And then she realized he'd probably been thinking about little else but her world since Hannah had been taken.

"How do you do it?" he asked. His voice was oddly soft now, and she felt as if he had put a gentle, reassuring hand on her shoulder.

"It must be done."

"At what cost?"

"Does that matter, if I find Hannah safe?"

"It must matter to you, the price you pay."

She fought down the memories that threatened to surge every time she thought of what Hannah and her friends could be going through. She focused instead on the deep, echoing strength of his voice. She found an odd sort of support in it and was able to speak almost evenly.

"If not me, who?"

"Someone who perhaps does not feel so deeply."

That was so pointed that for an instant she wondered who he'd been talking to. A possibility occurred to her.

"Been to the local doctor lately?"

Caleb blinked. One corner of his mouth twitched. And she knew her stab in the dark had struck home.

"So, my brother's been talking about me?"

"He merely mentioned in passing that he was worried about you."

"He does that. Worry, I mean."

"He is a very good doctor."

She found it explanation rather than non sequitur. And then she realized they had been talking easily, if not comfortably, for some time now. The house was quiet, the girls asleep, and the golden glow from the gas lamps was somehow comforting, soothing.

"The girls enjoyed having you here this evening. This is the first time since Hannah...was taken that they have truly laughed."

"I enjoyed them," she said. "I used to spend time playing games with my little sister and brother, and this took me back."

"I am glad you came."

She opened her mouth for the expected thanks for being invited, but the words wouldn't come. Because he was looking at her in a way that made it impossible to speak. If he was a man of her world, she would have thought... But he wasn't.

And she wasn't a woman of his.

For a moment the comfort of this quiet home, the warmth, the simplicity, pulled at her with a strength unlike anything she'd ever felt before. There was more to this life than just a quaint eccentricity. She'd spent an entire evening with her phone set on vibrate only, without television or radio, or earphones on, and she hadn't missed any of it. In fact, it had been a relief, if how relaxed she felt now was any indication.

Or at least, how relaxed she'd felt until Caleb had looked at her that way.

"Your girls," she said. "You're doing amazingly well with them."

"I have much help from the community."

She'd grown used to the occasional difference in cadence and sentences from him and the rest of the village, who all grew up speaking Pennsylvania Dutch, a German dialect, and only learned English when they started school, or from older siblings. She found it part of the charm and knew enough German to manage a few useful phrases herself.

She almost commented on the ulterior motives of the women in the community who were so helpful with his children but decided to stay quiet on that front. Not only because it seemed catty, but because she felt oddly reluctant to acknowledge that in the community, Caleb was quite a catch. There were women lined up for a chance at him.

"They're delightful girls," she said instead, keeping the focus on a safer topic. "Each so different."

He nodded. "Katie will be fine," he said. "She is gentle and kind, like her mother. Grace is too young to be certain yet, but she is also much like her mother."

The omission was obvious. Emma understood. "Ruthie will be fine, too."

"She is…unsettled."

"And unsettling?"

His mouth quirked. "That, as well."

She smiled at him. "She will be different, and she will likely make you want to tear your hair out on occasion, but she will be fine."

He gave her a look that made her wonder what he was thinking, made her suspect he was picturing another unsettling young girl.

"You speak from experience?"

"Let's just say my parents would empathize with you about Ruthie."

He laughed again. Better than the first time,

more solid, real, not quite so rusty. The smile he gave her then took her breath away.

"I feel I would have liked your parents."

"And they," she said, "would have liked you."

Silence spun out between them. On it went, like the fiber she'd seen an Amish woman spinning yesterday, growing tighter with each moment. She couldn't seem to look away, and he gave her no help, studying her as if she were some fascinating oddity dropped into his world.

She stood up abruptly. Looking surprised, he also stood. Emma's need to escape was strong, and only the little voice in her mind that accused her of running stopped her from bolting out the front door. The rudeness of that sparked a need to be gracious, as if to cover the impulse.

"Thank you. I had a wonderful evening."

Lord, she sounded like a woman after an awkward date. And that opened up her mind for images that she knew had to be quashed, instantly.

"I know the girls did, too," he said.

And you?

She clamped her teeth together to prevent the treacherous words from escaping. Had he purposely avoided including himself? She searched for something else, anything else to say. Something that would bring her stupidly rebellious mind back in line, slow her pulse back to normal.

What I need is a bucket of cold water, she thought.

And then she found it.

"I will find her," she said, bringing the reality of the reason she was here back to the fore with warmth-dispelling abruptness.

Caleb's face changed as if she had literally hit him with that cold splash. As if he, too, at least for a moment, had forgotten this wasn't just an ordinary social evening, that she wasn't just an invited guest in his home.

"I know that you will try to the fullest extent," he said, sounding as stiff as she felt.

She mumbled something else as she made her escape into the night. And it wasn't until she was clear of Paradise Ridge that her pulse returned to normal.

Her mind, however, seemed to have no such inclination.

Chapter 15

"Is Emma coming tonight?"

Caleb looked down at his middle daughter. Ruthie had put the question to him last night as well, as if Emma's presence were supposed to be a regular occurrence instead of a single event two nights ago.

A single, memorable event.

He tried to look at it rationally. He had greatly enjoyed seeing his daughters laughing and happy. Even little Grace had seemed fascinated by their guest, staring at her wide-eyed, one finger in her tiny mouth.

And Emma had been *their* guest. He appreciated that she had spent as much time playing with the girls, keeping up her end of the Scrabble game, as she had with him.

Once it had been them alone, she hadn't stayed long. He didn't know if it had been out of respect for proprieties, or if she simply wanted away from him. But he'd been both grateful and disappointed, and it was the latter that had him so unsettled now.

Because his daughter's eager question had brought him face-to-face with a fact he'd been trying to ignore. He had enjoyed that evening as much as the girls had. He had enjoyed watching the sharp, professional woman unbend and laugh, even giggle with them, watching her take on the challenge of the familiar game and the unfamiliar way of playing it, hearing her talk to the children with respect, not asking any of the questions so many outsiders did, about their lives and how they lived without the things that ruled her own world.

"Is she, Father?"

Jerked back to the present, Caleb focused on

the girl. "No, Ruthie. I have not seen her since she was here."

"If I see her, may I ask her to come?"

He hesitated, but then Katie chimed in. "Yes, please, Father, may we?"

This child, who was the living image of her mother, so rarely asked for anything that it wasn't in him to refuse her. Besides, what were the chances they would see the agent anyway?

"You may," he said, feeling fairly safe about it. Ruthie scampered off to finish preparing for school.

Emma had been busy, he knew that. Everyone in the village spoke of how she was relentless, coming back two, three times or even more to dig into their memories, trying to find one thing that might open up another lead. He assumed she had found nothing, or he would know by now. She had promised to keep him apprised of any developments.

Of course, that was likely what she always said; perhaps it had slipped her mind that she was not in a place where she could simply call to update him. He wondered briefly if a phone call from him to her, made at the community booth, would be permitted. He should have asked Deacon Stoltzfus the last time he was here to chastise him about his clean-shaven face.

Except the last time the Deacon was here, Hannah had been safe.

A memory shot through his mind, of the day Hannah was born. "You must always look out for your little sister, Caleb," his mother had said. True, she was an adult now, even in the eyes of the English, but to him, always meant always. And he hadn't done his job.

The wrenching worry he'd been living with threatened to break free. Hannah, lively, spirited Hannah, in the hands of evil. Who knew what might be happening to her at this very moment. He tamped it down yet again, although it was getting more difficult with every hour that passed with no news.

He shook his head, feeling as if it were filling with the fluffy fleece of the Yoders' sheep. He was not a man to sit and ponder while others did, and despite the common sense that told him Emma was trained for this, he felt strongly that he should be doing…something. And yet he knew Emma was right, that his place lay here, taking care of his girls. She would say so again, were she here.

For an instant he felt a tug so strong it shocked him, a need for just that, for the brusque, businesslike woman, who still could play with hurting children not even her own, to be here now. He told himself he needed to hear her telling him again it would be all right, she would bring his little sister home. And he couldn't deny he needed the reassurance.

But he also couldn't deny, were he to be truthful as a man should, that he wanted her here for other reasons. He wanted to feel again the pleasure of watching her smile, hearing her laugh, knowing she had allowed herself those feelings here. For he sensed that she rarely did, supposed that her world and her work didn't allow for that very often.

He wanted to watch the grace with which she

carried herself, the way her slender hands frequently moved to emphasize a point when she spoke. He even liked watching the bounce of her hair when she walked and had it in a ponytail.

Hair that, in his world, would have been bound up and covered, kept only for her husband's eyes.

A sensation of heat and aching hollowness burst through him, and he thought for an instant that he actually swayed on his feet.

"Father?"

Katie's soft voice pulled him out of the morass of tangled feelings he seemed to be mired in. He looked at her, at this child who so resembled her mother, and regained his steadiness.

"Are you all right?" she asked anxiously.

"I am fine."

"You looked…so pained, just now."

"I am fine," he said, not denying what had likely been obvious on his face. "Are you ready for school?"

"Yes. And Grace is dressed for Mrs. Stoltzfus."

Caleb smiled at his oldest daughter. Even though she had been only eight, the girl had taken it upon herself to carry much of the load of caring for the baby after Annie had died. He had feared he would have to deal with childish anger at the innocent babe whose arrival into the world had taken her mother's life. But Katie had instead embraced the helpless child, saying only that it would be her mother's wish, and that Grace must have been her mother's last task here on earth, and therefore very important.

Caleb had been humbled by her simple faith. He wondered if there were many men in the world who felt they should strive to be more like their own child.

"She is a better Christian than I," he had once said to Jacob Yoder, his closest friend in the village.

"Children often are," his wise friend had said. "It is so clear to them."

"While adults struggle?"

"I think the weight of growing up sometimes holds us down in the mire, where things aren't as clear."

For a farmer, Jacob was of a decidedly philosophical bent at times.

He should go visit his old friend, Caleb thought as he walked the girls to school after dropping Grace at Mrs. Stoltzfus's. The toddler had been in a chattering mood this morning, and the subject of the pretty woman she called "Gen Emma" in her effort to copy her sisters' "Agent Emma" had seemed to Caleb nearly constant. And it had struck him that he was holding in his arms the answer to the question of how the news of her evening spent at his home had spread so quickly.

Not that there was anything wrong about her visit. The people of Paradise Ridge often had English visitors. They had good relations, both business and personal, with their neighbors of Eden Falls, and they fostered them. It was a mutually beneficial arrangement. The Amish community, sometimes to their own discomfort, drew large numbers of tourists to the area, and the spillover benefited the merchants and other businesses of Eden Falls. In turn, the close proximity of the English town, with all the modern devices those tourists could not live without, kept most of them staying there during their visit.

Emma, he had noticed, had changed a setting on her cell phone the moment she had set foot in the house. It had remained silent all evening, although he'd noticed her glancing at it discreetly a couple of times. He supposed she had to be always in touch, and had thought it a very polite gesture that she silenced the ringing and didn't actually speak on it while she was in his home.

He could have told her that since she was English their rules didn't apply to her, but he appreciated the gesture too much to tell her it didn't matter.

And just like that he was back to the nagging, persistent thoughts of the woman who seemed determined to plague him without even trying.

With an effort he was not used to having to make, he forced his thoughts to the day ahead. He walked at an accelerated pace to his shop. Today he would put the final finish on the commissioned desk, a large piece topped with the last of the wonderfully grained wood he'd used on the display piece in the window. The seven drawers were finally done, the dovetail joints tight and solid, the slides perfectly smoothed. He would go over it once more, from all angles, slanting a light over it to reveal any imperfections, and then the finishing work would begin.

And it would, thankfully, require his full and concentrated attention. There would be no room in his head for unwanted, improper and verboten thoughts of a certain FBI agent.

Chapter 16

Emma let her head fall back on the headrest. She was tired. She could no longer deny it. She was nearly exhausted, not so much because her days had been long, although they had, but because they had been fruitless. She'd never run into so many dead ends, so many leads that went nowhere, such a lack of real clues or evidence.

And of course the dreams weren't helping. Her nights had been a tangled cacophony of good and evil, horrible memories of her own entwined with images from that evening at Caleb's. It was as if her brain was weary of dealing with the two extremes and threw them all into the bubbling brew of her subconscious, to escape and torment her when she finally gave in to sleep.

She told herself it was just her frustration that made this case seem so much more important than any other. The case she was on at the moment was always the most important at the time, but this one seemed to have assumed huge proportions in her mind. It had to do only with the lack of headway, she assured herself.

And nothing to do with Caleb and his charming, lovable family.

She never should have gone there the other night. It had been too nice. Too enjoyable.

Too personal.

Somewhere during that evening she'd crossed a line. Not overtly—she'd done or said nothing wrong—but in her mind, she knew she had stepped into an ethical and inward morass. Because in Caleb's house she had found what she had missed the most since striking out on her own and leaving the Double C. While she had missed the ranch, the space, the horses, the very land of her home, she missed the people the most, and the sense of family. Not that it wasn't still her home anytime she wanted, but it wasn't the same, even with Piper and Sawyer still there. It wasn't like it had been with Caleb and his girls that night.

And that, she told herself sternly, was the very reason she could not go back. She would keep him up-to-date, in a professional manner, but no more warm, cozy evenings. Of course, there was that cell-phone thing, which meant in order to keep him apprised she would have to see him face-to-face, but she would do it at his shop or somewhere else. The image of that quiet, solid house, full of golden light and family bonds, threatened to burrow into a heart she only now, after all this time, admitted was homesick for that feeling.

"So much for being an independent, career-minded woman," she muttered to herself. The fact that she was supposedly a tough, trained federal agent was something she didn't want to acknowledge just now.

She allowed herself a moment of rest, her

eyes closed, justifying it by forcing herself to go through it all again, every bit of knowledge she'd gleaned since she'd been here. It wouldn't take long, she thought ruefully, because there was so little. But she ran through it anyway.

Hannah, Rebecca and Miriam had helped plan the very party they'd disappeared from. Rebecca's family's barn had been chosen because it was large enough to contain everyone. The cooking and preparing had gone on for days beforehand. Among the girls anyway. The boys seemed only to have to show up, except for Rebecca's brothers and a couple of friends who built makeshift tables for the gathering. Eli, the oldest of these, had said he'd been so focused on spending an evening with Rachel Miller that he had paid scant attention to his sister and her friends. And his story was echoed by many others; some things, Emma thought, apparently including the single-mindedness of hormone-driven teenagers, crossed cultures.

But even the few adults around, the ones who had stayed near the house to let the youngsters have their day, hadn't seen anything different or unusual. No one had seen a stranger or strangers hanging around. She'd talked to everyone in Paradise Ridge old enough to communicate. Many she'd spoken to at the community meeting, but few had had anything useful to say; she spent most of her time reassuring them. Some she'd recontacted later, particularly those who had been near the party or who lived close by.

Over the past couple of days, she'd expanded to people who were known but not part of the community, people they had contact with on at least a semiregular basis. And still nothing. No mysterious activity, no strangers about, no unknown vehicles, nothing.

She was missing something. She had to be.

She believed Caleb when he'd said Hannah would not leave of her own volition without saying goodbye to the girls. The family was too close-knit, and from everything the girls had told her, Hannah was too loving a soul to be that cold and unthinking.

She hadn't really thought it was that anyway.

Her every instinct told her this was an abduction, not a runaway. If for no other reason than why would they run away during this time when they were allowed to explore outside the community without censure? Simply put, she thought, they didn't *have* to run away to the outside world; they could just go, so why would they?

She let out a long, weary breath. Yes, she was definitely missing something. An abduction, but no strangers around, no strange vehicles—for there almost had to be one involved, given how completely and quickly the three girls had vanished—noticed, nothing. And those same instincts told her no one from within the community was involved, and nothing she'd seen or heard in her interviews had changed that feeling.

An abduction.

No strangers.

No one on the inside.

Emma went very still. She kept her eyes closed, not wanting to disrupt the turn her thoughts had taken.

Turn it around, she said to herself.

Not a stranger, but someone known to them.

But yet, not on the inside.

A tap on the truck's window jolted her upright. If this were Cleveland, Tate's Philly or any other big city, she could have been dead, zoning out like that. Angry with herself, she turned her head. And saw the top of a slightly askew Amish cap.

She rolled down the window, and the cap tilted back.

"Ruthie!" she exclaimed. "What are you doing here and not in school?"

The girl's nose wrinkled. "It's Saturday, Agent Emma. I'm taking my father his lunch."

She lifted a cloth sack. Emma stared at it, trying to process the fact that she had completely lost track of what day it was. Derek would say she was working too hard. To Caleb and the others in this community, she wasn't sure there was such a thing as working too hard. The Amish work ethic was legend, but until now, when she'd spent so much time here at a stretch, she hadn't realized how very true it was. The farmers among them kept the same long hours that had been their way, by necessity, since they'd first established their little community.

Caleb's days were a little more reasonable, or at least he had made them that way so he could see the girls off in the mornings. She liked that he'd made that adjustment for them.

She gestured to Ruthie, who backed up so she could open the door. She slid out and closed the truck door. The moment it was shut, the girl spoke.

"Come to dinner tonight."

Emma blinked. Temptation came in many unexpected forms, but she'd never expected to see it in the shape of a seven-year-old Amish girl.

"I can't, Ruthie," she said, startled despite her earlier self-acknowledgment at how much she wished she could say yes.

"Father said I could invite you."

She stared down at the determined child. She knew the child likely wouldn't lie, and yet she'd had the feeling that, at the end of that wonderful evening, Caleb had been as glad to see her go as she had been to escape.

"He did?" Emma asked, unable to stop herself.

Ruthie nodded vigorously, her cap bobbing. "He said if I saw you, I could invite you."

Ah, she thought. It was the qualifier that no doubt had Caleb feeling safe. Although, she thought perhaps he underestimated his energetic middle child; she had a feeling once she had that okay, Ruthie would make sure she somehow saw Emma so she could extend the invitation.

"I'm flattered," Emma said, meaning it. "Truly. But it's not…appropriate."

Ruthie frowned. "But you must eat. And it's Saturday."

"I'm working," she said. It was automatic, a reflex; she hadn't had much to work on for two days now. Her time had been spent simply recovering old ground. It was as if the girls had been snatched up by invisible aliens, vanishing literally without a trace.

"English don't work on Saturday," Ruthie pointed out.

Feeling a bit desperate, Emma pointed at the sack the girl held. "Your father's working."

"But he always does." The girl's expression changed, the furrow between her brows giving her a worried look. "He says he needs to catch up. He's worried about Aunt Hannah."

"I know," Emma said softly. "And I know you are, too."

"No," Ruthie said, startling her.

"You're not worried?"

"You'll find her," Ruthie said confidently. "I know you will."

Emma would have appreciated the complete faith a bit more had she the slightest idea where she was going to turn next. The last time she talked to Tate, he seemed to think he had something worth checking out, and that was the closest they had to any kind of lead.

"Come with me, at least," Ruthie said, gesturing with the food she was to deliver. "Father is wondering when there will be news."

"I'm sure he is," Emma said with an inward grimace. *So am I,* she added silently. If something didn't break soon, she was going to call for help. Not that her boss in Cleveland would appreciate that; he would think she should be back there working their own cases. He'd okayed her to come see if there was a connection, not work to solve a Pennsylvania case for them. So far she'd successfully stalled him off by citing the similarities between this case and their own, but she didn't know how long that was going to work.

"Come," Ruthie insisted. Then the girl took Emma's hand and tugged. And after a moment of resistance that would have to have been stronger to be deemed even token, Emma thought sourly, she gave in. She should check in with him anyway, and better his shop than going back to that tempting, luring home.

She reached back to grab the truck's keys and locked the door; it was in no danger from the locals, of course, but with no snow there were still a few tourists lingering this late in the year, and where there were tourists there were opportunists.

Emma heard the steady sound of a motor as they neared the old building Caleb had taken over as his shop. Today the generator was running. When they stepped into the shop, she smelled the sharp, heady odor of some kind of paint. Involuntarily she sniffed.

"It's what my father puts on the wood to protect it."

Emma smiled at the girl's quick response to a question she hadn't even asked. Apparently she'd inherited her father's perceptiveness.

"He finished a big desk yesterday. It's in the drying room now. That's why the generator's running. There are heat lamps in there. Usually he only uses it to run the air compressor for the air tools when he needs them. The saws and sanders."

"You're better than a tour guide," Emma teased. Ruthie grinned, and once more Emma wondered how that irrepressible spirit would manage in this quiet, controlled world. Would Caleb be as wise as her own parents had been with her, seeing that she needed to run free sometimes to enable her to stay within the lines the rest of the time?

They found him in the office area at the back of the shop, standing before a large drafting table. There was a big window in the west-facing wall the table stood against, providing a full flood of light, negating for the moment at least the need for any other source.

Ruthie ran over to her father.

"I brought your lunch," she said. "And something better."

"So I see."

Caleb took the sack and set it on the table that apparently served as a desk. He seemed inordinately intent on making certain it was placed so it didn't fall off.

"I invited her to dinner. You said I could," Ruthie reminded him when his gaze narrowed.

"So I did."

She couldn't read anything into his tone. Apparently neither could Ruthie, because the child chattered on easily.

"Katie will make biscuits, and we have the

beef stew Mrs. Yoder made." She looked at Emma. "Do you like beef stew?"

"Love it," she answered, although the idea of declaring herself allergic and backing out as gracefully as possible occurred to her; Caleb did not look any happier than she was feeling about this.

"*Daed,*" Ruthie said again, giving it the Pennsylvania Dutch pronunciation, "is making some shelves for Mrs. Yoder, for her quilting things. So she makes extra for us when she cooks her own dinner three times a week."

"Sounds like an equitable bargain," Emma said, keeping her gaze on the voluble child and away from her taciturn father.

"Equi— What does that mean?"

"What does it sound like?" Caleb asked before Emma could answer.

Ruthie frowned, apparently working it out. Emma guessed this was a frequent happening, not giving the easy answer but making her think it through. She remembered her own father doing the same to her.

"It sounds sort of like equal," Ruthie said.

"Yes," Caleb said with an encouraging nod.

"So does it mean a bargain where both sides are equal? A fair bargain?"

Caleb smiled. "That's my clever girl."

Ruthie beamed. The girl practically glowed. Emma remembered the feeling, when a smile and unstinting approval from her father made her world warm and right.

"May I go look at the desk?" she asked.

"Only through the window."

"I know. Dust."

The girl scampered off. Emma watched her go with a smile she couldn't help.

"She amuses you?"

"Yes." She gave him a sideways glance. "And she still reminds me of me at that age."

"Then she will grow out of…the more trying aspects?"

Emma analyzed that for a moment, wondering if it was compliment or accusation.

"Some," she finally said. "As long as you don't try to crush them out of her."

"I have no wish to crush her spirit, though some say I should. It's a parent's job to channel it."

She couldn't argue with that. And winced at the idea of trying to break Ruthie's energetic spirit. "She'll learn to restrain it when required. But when she finds her passion, she'll be hard to stop," Emma said, wondering what would happen if that passion turned out to be something not acceptable in their world.

Caleb sighed. "She is much like Hannah," he said.

In that unguarded moment Emma saw the deep, gnawing concern he kept so well masked the rest of the time, for the girls' sake, she supposed. He was worried about his sister. Very worried. Just because he was not of her world didn't mean he wasn't aware of the dangers. The opposite, in fact; the dangers were part of the reason he was apart from it.

"There is no news?" he asked, his voice tight.

"I would have told you immediately," she said, regretful that she had nothing hopeful to share.

He merely nodded, absorbing the blow with the stoicism and acceptance of his kind. Yet she could see the pain in his face, see the shadow haunting his eyes, those amazing eyes. She wanted to go to him, to reassure him, hold him until that look left his eyes.

But she could do none of that. Not that it wasn't part of her job, reassuring stressed-out relatives, but she didn't dare get so close to this man.

And oddly, as if he somehow knew what she was thinking, he took a step back, away from her. But something else flashed in his eyes for an instant, and she dared to wonder if these tangled feelings were not one-sided.

It should have soothed her restlessness, to know he was feeling it, too, and would be as on guard as she was.

Instead, it made her heart leap with a joy she couldn't quite quash.

And that scared her more than anything.

Chapter 17

It had to stop, Emma thought.

She couldn't risk this again. She couldn't give in again to the temptations of another pleasant evening with Caleb and his girls.

Pleasant. What a weak-sounding word for what she'd felt tonight. Too weak for the enjoyment she'd had watching the interaction between the girls, even little Grace, who was overcoming her awe of "Gen Emma" and joining in the chatter in her sometimes nonsensical way or in Pennsylvania Dutch too fast for Emma to follow. Too weak for the too-long-unaccustomed joy of laughing until she nearly wept.

Too weak for the heady feeling she got every time she caught Caleb's gaze on her.

And far, far too weak for the sensation that rippled through her when she thought—for surely she must have imagined it—she saw a heat in his eyes that echoed what he seemed able to trigger in her with the slightest glance.

It was impossible, of course. She knew that. Likely her imagination. And even if it wasn't, it was still impossible. Her world, his world…no matter how appealing she might find the idea of his simpler, plainer life, the two couldn't mix. It had to be one or the other.

And that she was even allowing the possibility of such a choice to enter her mind rattled her to her core.

She watched the now-familiar bedtime preparations for the girls, marveling at how obedient they were, even the fiery Ruthie going with minimal protest. Her world could learn much from this one, she thought. And there it was again.

She spent the moments while Caleb tended to his daughters, with a gentle care that made her ache somewhere deep inside, steeling herself, reinforcing barriers she'd never had to worry so much about before. It wasn't that she didn't always feel a personal connection to the people of her cases; she did, she felt their pain and distress, and developing a rapport with people was as much a part of her job as anything else.

But rapport was not what she was feeling with Caleb Troyer.

But it had to be. And that's all it could be. And it was time—past time—for her to get back to business. And only business.

By the time he came back, she had the walls back up and reinforced. It wasn't that the sight of him, the easy way he moved, the lovely gray of his eyes, the power and strength of his hands and the gentle way he used them, didn't still send her senses careening; it was that she'd determined, with a fierce, Colton stubbornness, that she wasn't going to give in to it.

And more importantly, that she wasn't going to let it show.

He took the chair opposite her. He studied her

for a moment, and Emma steadfastly quashed the leap of her pulse.

"You had something you wished to say or ask?"

How did he do that? she wondered. She'd said nothing about needing to talk to him or question him, yet he had obviously sensed it.

It doesn't matter, she told herself. She was through with speculation of that kind. It was time to get this investigation back on a professional footing. And if that meant constant vigilance over her own foolish reactions anytime she was in this man's presence, then so be it.

"Yes," she said, her voice sounding a little abrupt. She didn't apologize—better to seem abrupt than a quivering puddle.

Quickly, she brought him up-to-date. Not that there was much to tell, and she didn't bother to try and hide her growing frustration.

"Is there anyone you can think of that I should talk to that I haven't?"

He considered a moment, then shook his head. "From what I have heard, you've missed no one."

Now, there's a reminder, she thought; a community didn't need phones to have an effective and rapid grapevine.

"You're still sure there's no one in the outside community who could possibly have a grudge or who paid inordinate attention to Hannah or the others?"

"Is this what you do? Ask the same questions of the same people?"

It wasn't the first time she'd heard the accusation, although Caleb veiled it better than most; he'd sounded merely curious. It was, however, the first time in a long time that it had stung.

"Yes," she said, working to keep her tone even as she gave him a much longer explanation than she usually did. "Often, the first time you ask, people answer without thinking. But you've planted the idea, and their conscious and subconscious mind go to work on it. They're thinking about it, even if they're not aware of it. Going back and asking again sometimes gets us answers the person would have sworn they didn't know the first time we asked."

He nodded, unruffled, as if he had indeed been merely curious when he'd asked. Perhaps he had been, she thought, and it was her own unsettled mental state around him that had made her read more into it.

"We are honest in our dealings, so there are few disputes that would lead to that kind of anger," he said. "As for the other…Hannah in particular is a beautiful young woman. Beautiful enough that the elders have always been concerned, lest she become too proud of that beauty."

He paused, giving her a look that seemed almost hesitant.

"That must seem strange to you. Your world seems to prize beauty above all."

"My world, maybe. My family? Not a chance."

He blinked, drew back slightly. "Oh?"

"My father always hammered it into us that a less-than-perfect woman with a good brain was infinitely more attractive than a perfect beauty with nothing but air behind her eyes."

A slow smile curved his mouth. That wonderful, tempting mouth.

"I believe I would have liked your father."

"And he you."

"And his worries were clearly unnecessary."

It was her turn to blink. "What?"

"You became both."

It was the most subtly delivered yet obviously sincere compliment she'd ever gotten. And it was so unexpected she very much feared she was gaping at him like a landed fish. She felt the sudden urge to run, to dash away to somewhere quiet where she could think. Where she could turn it over and around in her mind and figure out if it meant that perhaps she hadn't been completely fanciful in thinking there had, more than once, been an answering heat in his eyes, an echoing of the churning that began in her every time she was in the presence of this man.

But she had made a vow to herself, and she was going to keep it. She was going to focus on the case and nothing else. She had to.

"Thank you," she managed, not letting herself think about how long she'd likely been staring at him. And trying to sound as if she got compliments all the time. Which, when she took the time and trouble to pull herself together, she often did. But she found she appreciated the extra time minimum attention to her appearance gave her, so rare was the occasion that bestirred her to get out the face paint and lipstick, as Piper called it.

"This is also a repeat question," she began, knowing she sounded abrupt this time, but continuing without apology. "You are absolutely certain there is no one within the community who would—"

"Yes. No one."

"No spurned suitors, or—"

"No."

Emma wondered what it was like to have such utter faith in your fellow man. But she needed him to think, to truly think, of things he might find impossible to fathom. She hated that she had to do it, but there was no avoiding it.

"Your sister's life could depend on you being brutally honest."

This time it was he who explained. "Were it only Hannah, there might be. She had boys enough after her. But if it was that, why the other girls?"

He'd put his finger on it, the detail she'd come back to repeatedly herself, one that had pointed her in the direction she was now heading. But first she had to make sure she'd eliminated every other possibility.

"Boys enough?" she asked.

He nodded. "But she was interested in none of them, so there was no one who could take offense over another. It was understood that she simply wasn't ready to settle down."

Others had told her much the same thing, that Hannah Troyer had been in no hurry to select a mate and begin life in the community she'd grown up in. As appealing as she herself was finding the simplicity of this life, she doubted it would be drawing her as it was if she hadn't spent the rest of her life out in the wider world.

Was that Hannah's problem? Was she drawn to what Emma herself had grown up with, and now found herself wishing she could escape?

It was yet another effort to rechannel her thoughts yet again. Focus, she ordered herself.

"All right, Caleb," she said, by now forgoing the formal "Mr. Troyer" without even thinking. "Say we accept it's not someone in the community, nor anyone on the edges, that you deal with. And if it's not a stranger—"

"A stranger out there would likely have been noticed, yes," he said. His voice was soft, taking on an almost husky note. She didn't dare let herself speculate on why, afraid she'd convince herself it was simply because she'd said his name.

Determinedly, she kept going. "Then that leaves someone else."

"If you eliminate people we know and strangers, what is left?" he asked, his brows raised.

"Someone who's both," she said.

Chapter 18

Emma was angry that it had taken her a few days to work her way around to this. The fact that a stranger abduction was the most logical didn't mean she could ignore other possibilities. Even though the retention rate in the Amish community was high, a few people did leave.

She supposed she'd just gotten it into her head that if anyone left, it would be a difficult decision, abandoning all they'd ever known, leaving this peaceful, calm life for the frenetic "other" world. And that they would leave either regretfully or eagerly, but not angrily or with hatred for their family or the way they lived.

"You're letting your own feelings color this," she muttered to herself.

Just because she was feeling the pull of this quiet, unruffled existence didn't mean it wasn't anathema to others, even—or perhaps especially—some of those who had grown up with it. And that quiet, unruffled existence was still peopled by humans, with all their failings and some of the same problems the outside world had.

She guessed a psychopath could just as easily be born Amish. Which would be a great study for some shrink arguing the nature-versus-nurture case.

She reined her mind back in, irritated anew; she'd never been prone to wandering, philosophical thoughts like this, and she didn't have time for it now. She looked at the mostly checked-off list she held. Last night Caleb had given her a couple of names, but said he was sure there were more he didn't know. Emma would have thought the decision of a child to leave would have been big news in the small community, and was at first surprised Caleb hadn't been able to name them all off himself.

"Ones in the past, yes," he'd said quietly. "In the last three years, no."

She'd felt herself flush, embarrassed that she hadn't realized what should have been clear— Caleb hadn't been paying much attention to anything but his own pain since the death of his wife. And as always, that was the one thing that could throw cold water on her silly reaction to him.

He had told her Mrs. Stoltzfus was her best source; she would know not only who had left but why and if they were still in touch with their family here, how often and just about everything they'd done since leaving. Every community, it seemed, had its information clearinghouse. And Mrs. Stoltzfus indeed had had all the information she could want.

So she'd spent today, armed with more details than she could remember at the moment, once more making rounds, stopping to talk with families who had lost one to the outside world.

She had expected reluctance to speak of the lost one, and she'd been right so far; it had been like pulling out splinters, especially compared to the voluble Mrs. Stoltzfus. But no matter how disappointed they were in the person's decision, none of them could even begin to take seriously that they would do such a thing.

"Those Ohio Amish, from where you are, perhaps," one matron told her now, rather stiffly, despite Emma's effort to explain she was merely exploring other avenues. "But not here. And not my Solomon."

So, Emma thought as she thanked Mrs. Miller for her cooperation—which in fact had been more than lacking—and made her escape, was there really a social-order system of sorts among the greater Amish community? Did one think of itself as more observant than another and therefore more worthy?

Or was it simply that there were women like Mrs. Miller in every community, Amish or not?

Emma smiled to herself as she headed back to the ranch truck. Some things, it seemed, were indeed universal, including some personality types. Perhaps her precious Solomon had had good reason to leave that had little to do with his life here and much to do with his mother.

Even during the short time she'd been inside this last house, it had gone from afternoon to dark with the speed of this time of year. And just as quickly it had gone from brisk to downright cold, and she hastened her steps, glad the truck had a very efficient heater.

She was warm by the time she reached the main street of Paradise Ridge. It was already closing down, but the lamps were still on in the bakery, and on impulse she stopped. She would take a pie home to the ranch, she thought. It would be welcomed, and she could kid herself into thinking it was just the food and warmth that had made her feel so welcome in Caleb's home.

The young woman behind the counter was as gracious and smiling as Mrs. Miller had been grim and forbidding. Emma smiled back, placing her as the daughter of the woman who normally ran the bakery, who was also Mrs. Miller. Mrs. Miller number one, Emma thought, to differentiate the much more kindly woman from the Mrs. Miller number two she'd talked to earlier today.

The girl quickly boxed up the Dutch apple Emma picked out, and tucked in an extra couple of turnovers as well, saying as her last customer of the day, she might as well take them with her so they wouldn't be discarded.

"Thank you. Leah, isn't it?"

"Yes. And you're…Agent Colton?" The woman's smile faltered as she acknowledged Emma was no ordinary customer. When she had to reluctantly tell her there was no news on the missing girls, Emma felt that knot in her stomach that was growing every day. She'd been here less than a week, true, but she felt she'd made absolutely no progress. Just as back home in Ohio, whoever had done this had done it quickly, efficiently and without any fuss to draw attention.

And the fact that the Amish were so isolated,

so used to dealing with their own problems and avoiding outsiders, didn't help any.

Emma glanced outside into the darkness. "How are you getting home?" she asked the young woman. She was older than the targets had been so far, but not by much, and she was pretty. And alone.

"Walking, of course," she answered, sounding surprised. "I only live two blocks down."

Emma knew the answer would have been the same if the distance had been miles. "Let me walk with you."

"Oh, surely it will be all right. It's so close."

"But it's dark, and better to be safe."

The flash of gratitude in the young woman's eyes told Emma she'd guessed right. The undercurrent of fear in Paradise Ridge had by now reached all corners and was powerful enough to batter against the walls of faith that kept this community strong.

She set the bakery box in the truck, then waited while Leah turned out the lamps, covered the counters and locked up. Emma had talked to her briefly at the meeting, but she'd been with her parents, and beyond having known Hannah, she had had little to say.

"I'm sorry there's no news yet," she said as they started to walk. "I know Hannah was a friend of yours."

"I knew her," the girl said, as she had before. "But she's younger than I. Actually, I looked after her now and then when she was a child."

"Really? What was she like?"

Leah gave her a sideways look. Emma saw the hesitation there.

"It can't hurt, and it might help," she said quietly.

With a little sigh Leah went on. "She was… rebellious. No, that sounds too strong, and she was too kind to be angry. She was…"

"Restless?" Emma suggested.

"Yes," the girl said with relief. "That's it." Again she hesitated, but this time went on without prompting. "I always thought if anyone would choose the world of the English, it would be Hannah."

"Do you think that's what she did?"

"No," Leah said quickly. "Not like that. She would never leave the girls without a word. Her nieces. She adores them. Especially little Grace. She was practically her mother after—" she ducked her eyes hastily "—Mrs. Troyer died."

Emma didn't miss the telling dodge of the eyes and mentally added Leah to the list of young women with their eye on Caleb.

Can you blame them? she thought. *Did you really think you were the only one he has this effect on?*

"Did you know Miriam and Rebecca?"

"I knew them, of course. We all know each other. But they're even younger than Hannah, so they were…just kids."

Emma nodded in understanding as they neared the small, tidy house with a freshly painted fence, a neat garden now lying fallow for the winter except for a few late crops and the now-familiar warm, golden glow of the gas lamps in the window.

"I'm sorry I can't help," Leah said.

She sounded miserable, and Emma reassured her quickly. "Don't be. It's perfectly normal that you spend most of your time with people your own age. And you have your own family to focus on."

"Seven brothers," she said, and Emma thought there was a wry note in her voice.

"I have four," Emma said with an empathetic laugh. "I know what you mean."

On that companionable note they parted, although Emma, after declining the tentative offer to come inside for something warm to drink, waited until the girl was safely inside. Then she turned and started back toward the truck, once more turning it all over in her mind, wondering if at last she'd found the right direction, if perhaps someone who was known and yet no longer known was the key to it all.

She had the truck unlocked and was sliding into the driver's seat before she noticed the slip of paper under the windshield wiper. She got out again to look, saw that it was a torn strip of lined paper like that used in spiral notebooks everywhere. She reached for it, then stopped. She leaned back into the truck and reached for her kit, a small aluminum case that went everywhere and contained, among other things, a minimal evidence kit. She grabbed a pair of latex gloves, snapped them on, picked out a small, flat plastic ziplock bag, then reached for the note.

And nearly dropped it the moment she looked at it.

Emma felt her knees wobble. She grasped for some rational thought, some way for this not to be what it looked like, but her brain had locked, and her own voice was screaming so loudly in her head she wasn't at all sure she wasn't letting it out into the suddenly frigid air.

The words seemed to almost dance on the ripped page, taunting, swirling, laughing at her, the odd rows of numbers along the edges seeming to spin in place.

The words. She stared at them.

Must I be a Christian child,

Gentle patient meek and mild?

Oh yes, I must cheerfully obey

Giving up my will and way.

I must.

I must.

The words, she thought desperately. She'd seen them before. Or some form of them. The image of a verse posted in the schoolroom where the community meeting had been flashed through her mind. A nursery rhyme, almost the same words as these, yet commanding, not questioning as this did.

A nursery rhyme, twisted and broken to mean something entirely different.

Another fractured nursery rhyme. Written in a child's crayon. Just like the other.

A chill deeper than any winter seized her, as if an arctic blast had swept in. Deeper because this chill came from inside, from that deep, buried place where she kept the memories of those nine eternal days of hell she'd endured at the hands of the monster she refused to honor with a name.

She tried to focus, tried over and over to tell herself it couldn't be, it simply couldn't be. The numbers, those were different. The writing itself was different. It couldn't be.

But it could be. Hadn't she lived with that fear from the moment she'd gotten notice that her nightmare was going to be set loose? Hadn't her anger nearly consumed her, no matter how often Tate had told her it was just the way the system, too often, didn't work? His words hadn't worked then, and they wouldn't work now. Because now she felt no anger, only that icy cold.

So cold she was surprised her heart kept beating. So cold she doubted she would ever be warm again. She felt as if something was quaking deep inside her, some tiny bit of humanity that was curling in on itself, preparing to die.

She didn't know what to do. She was a highly trained federal agent, she'd dealt with criminals of every evil stripe, and yet now she stood here, helpless, too frozen to move. It was dark and quiet here in Paradise Ridge at this hour; there was no one to call out to, if she could even find her voice.

She realized she was shaking, that inward cold

gripping harder. She tried to move, tried to use that skill of compartmentalization that had enabled her to keep going in the face of horrors most people would never see.

She couldn't. She couldn't shove the evil back into it's cage. It was too strong and right now she too weak to deal. Tate would tell her to man up and get past it, but he'd always given her credit for more strength than she'd ever really believed she had. It wasn't Tate's bracing words she wanted.

She didn't want to freeze to death standing here.

She just wanted to be warm again.

Chapter 19

Caleb had been staring at the same page for... he didn't know exactly how long. It wasn't that the book wasn't interesting. It was; he favored historical biographies, liked to know about other lives in other places, even if he would never experience either firsthand. But he was having trouble concentrating, and after reading one page repeatedly and still having absorbed little of it, he finally leaned back in his chair and closed his eyes for a moment.

The girls were settled in bed. They'd eaten well tonight, thanks to Mrs. Yoder's contribution of a roasted chicken. The meal had been a quiet one. The girls were becoming more and more concerned about their beloved aunt, and Caleb knew his own deepening worry was affecting them. Just as it was poking at him, prodding at him, telling him he should be doing something, not just sitting here waiting for outsiders to find her.

And yet what choice did he have? He had the girls to take care of, and he had no idea how to do any more than had already been done. He'd done his share of hunting; he could follow a trail, if there was one to follow. But there wasn't.

And that realization, along with his growing fear that Hannah might never be found, had pushed him into near silence tonight. The entire evening had been a marked contrast to the lively chatter that had gone on when Emma had joined them. He told himself he preferred the quiet, but he couldn't help remembering the way the girls had smiled and laughed the entire time she'd been with them.

He couldn't help remembering the way *he* had smiled and laughed the entire time she'd been with them.

His eyes snapped open and he shook his head sharply. Perhaps he should go to bed if he was so weary he couldn't keep control of his thoughts. Of course, in sleep all controls slipped, and no one knew that better than he. For months after Annie's death, his nights had been haunted by her image. Images that the most fervent prayers had been unable to stop.

And now they were haunted anew, fleeting dreams of an auburn-haired Englishwoman who tempted his soul, and he hated it.

Except that he didn't.

He heard the sounds of someone on the gravel walkway. He glanced at the clock on the shelf across the room. The old, steady heirloom that had been his grandfather's, and which was wound carefully every night, read a quarter to nine, late for callers. People rose early here, and it wasn't like them—

He slapped the book closed with a snap.

It wasn't like them, so it must be someone else.

"Emma," he breathed, surging to his feet with

an eagerness that embarrassed him once he realized where his mind had leaped.

He made himself walk slowly to the door. Or thought he did; there had still been no knock by the time he reached it. Yet he was certain he'd heard footsteps on the porch. Curious, and a little wary, he opened the door.

Light from inside spilled out onto the porch. The very woman who had so invaded his thoughts was standing there. The light caught the fire of her hair, and his reaction reminded him anew of why the women of his world wore coverings; this rich, thick fall of hair was definitely an adornment.

She looked up. Her eyes were wide and dark, and so full of dread it sent a shiver through him. And then he realized that *she* was shivering, from head to toe, shaking as if it were much, much colder than it actually was.

"Emma," he said.

She just stared at him with those eyes. His breath caught.

"Hannah?" he whispered, fearing the absolute worst.

For a moment she didn't react, as if she were having trouble processing. Then she shook her head, relieving that fear at least.

But doing nothing to explain why she was here and in such a state.

"Emma," he said again, "what's wrong?"

"I—"

Her teeth were chattering. He looked closer; the only way he could think of for her to be this cold was if she'd gotten soaked somehow or had been outside too long without a coat. But she wore the dark blue parka he'd seen before, and she appeared to be dry. Yet still she shivered and seemed too cold to even speak.

Finally galvanized, he moved. He stepped out and put his arm around her, urging her inside. He resisted, with some difficulty, the urge to simply take her in his arms and warm her with his own heat, since it had spiked as usual at the sight of her.

While she stood, shaking, he grabbed one of

the big upholstered chairs and pulled it over next to the woodstove. He'd been letting the fire dwindle while he'd tried to read, but he stoked it back up now, adding two pieces of well-seasoned wood that caught quickly.

He sat Emma in the chair—and she let him, without protest, which told him much about her state of mind—then walked to a trunk that sat against the far wall, opened it and took out a thick blue blanket. He came back and wrapped it around her. Then he pulled up a wood chair from the table and sat opposite her, waiting.

She looked around, but rather wildly, as if she were unable to focus on any one thing. But finally her eyes lit on the device that sat atop the woodstove. She seemed to focus on it, and Caleb seized the chance for distraction.

"It is a thermoelectric fan," he said. "It uses the Seebeck effect."

She blinked. Seeing she had at least stopped the wild glances, he went on, purposely making his voice as low and calm as he could.

"A German physicist, John Seebeck discovered in 1821 that when two metals that respond to heat at a different rate were placed near each other, it creates a small electric current along with a magnetic field."

Her brow was furrowed now as she looked at the fan, as if she were only now noticing that there was no outside power source or even a switch to indicate battery power.

He droned on, since his distraction appeared to be working. "That small current is enough to turn the blades when the stove gets warm enough. When the stove cools, it stops."

"An electric fan not plugged into electricity," she murmured.

"Exactly."

"Clever man, Mr. Seebeck."

"Yes."

"Handy, if you don't have electricity."

"Yes."

He waited a moment. It seemed the shivering had stopped, so he dared to ask again.

"What is wrong?"

"I…"

She paused, reached under the blanket and into her pocket to pull something out. It was a small plastic bag, sealed at the top, with writing across the seal in what he guessed was her bold yet feminine hand. Inside the bag was a torn piece of paper, perhaps six inches across. She held it out to him.

He hesitated, seeing now the word *evidence* printed at the top of the label. But still she held it out, so he reached for it. Their fingers brushed, and he felt a charge as definite as the one that powered the fan he'd explained to her. He barely managed not to jerk his hand away. He took the bag somewhat gingerly and looked at the paper it held.

He frowned. "This is a mangling of an old Amish children's verse," he said.

"I know. I saw it at the schoolhouse."

Her voice was steady enough, and her teeth were no longer chattering. But she did not, he noticed, let go of the blanket.

"What are the numbers?" he asked.

"I'm not sure."

Caleb felt at a loss. Emma was a strong woman, a very strong woman, and that she was so shaken by this surprised him. Her world was sometimes beyond comprehension, it seemed to him. The words and numbers scrawled in crayon made literal sense, but the meaning? He had no idea. But obviously she did; why else would it have put her into such a state?

"Does this have something to do with Hannah? With the other girls?"

"I... Maybe. I don't know."

"Something else, then?"

"Maybe."

"Emma," he said gently, "tell me what it is."

A renewed shiver rippled visibly through her. But after a moment she began to speak, choppily, in oddly disjointed sentences that gradually came together to form a picture of such horror his very spirit recoiled at it. A serial rapist with a sadistic streak who had taunted officials back in Ohio with notes very like this one, scribbled in crayon, with fractured nursery rhymes. A rapist who had taken and tortured a string of women from age twenty to sixty.

Caleb again fought the urge to reach for her, to hold her, comfort her. Her face was pale, drawn, her eyes still wide and haunted. He waited and, when she didn't go on, prompted her quietly. "And?"

"Then he took a thirteen-year-old girl."

Thirteen. One year older than his sweet, innocent Katie would be in just a few months. A fierce anger welled up in him. He tried to fight it but knew it was hopeless. God would just have to forgive him this time.

"I found him a week later."

"Of course you did," Caleb said, knowing deep inside that she would never, ever have quit until she did.

"He'd cut her. Badly. Worse than he'd meant to, I think."

Caleb suppressed a shiver of his own. Emma swallowed, and he saw her fingers curl, tightening on the edge of the blanket.

"She was dying. He'd been working on her for

a week, the longest yet. He loved knives. She needed medical attention immediately."

With her every word the urge in him grew to grab her, hold her, pull her away from the evil she dealt with every day. He was under no illusion; he knew her world desperately needed people like her, to deal with the scum like the man she spoke of. But he fiercely, desperately didn't want it to be her.

And he didn't want to know, but felt compelled to ask anyway.

"What happened?"

Emma stared down at the blanket, touching it with her fingers, as if she needed the contact with something real and now to survive the memories of then.

"She survived. She's still recovering, as best she can."

"You convinced him to let her be helped?"

"Sort of."

He waited a long moment before saying, "Emma?"

"I made a trade with him."

"A trade? What kind of trade?"

"The girl got help, got to a hospital."

"And he got…?"

"Me."

Chapter 20

Emma felt drained. She had never told it, not like that, not since the days of the investigation, and certainly not to a civilian. Yet it had come pouring out, as if Caleb had somehow found the safety valve and released it. As if, along with his apparent ability to send her body into overdrive, he also had found the way into her mind, as easily as he found the best grain of the wood he shaped.

"—yourself?"

She had to force herself to focus, to keep trying to swim upward out of the scalding sea of memories.

"What?"

If she had the strength, she'd be embarrassed by the faintness of her voice. She thought she'd had all this buried so deeply it would never surface again, and yet here she was, swamped anew as if it had happened two days ago, not two years.

"You sacrificed yourself to this...monster?"

Even through the fog she felt a little jolt as he chose the exact word she used herself. Or perhaps it was at the odd note his voice had taken on, as if his horror wasn't only at the existence of such creatures or even that a trade had been made, but that it was she who had made it.

"I... There was no choice." She didn't, couldn't look at him. She just kept touching the blanket. The soft feel of it was soothing, or maybe it was just that it had been Caleb who put it around her. "She was already dying, horribly, and he was about to finish it."

"So you offered him a fresh victim?"

"He'd already been taunting me, toying with me from the moment I found him with the girl. I thought the idea might intrigue him enough."

She gave a self-effacing half shrug. "My job was to save her."

"Your job." He sounded almost harsh. "Are there…many who would do what you did?"

She looked at him then. "Yes. There are. Not all outsiders accept our world as it is now."

"This is why you do what you do?"

"In part, yes."

"How long?"

She knew he wasn't asking how long she'd been on the job, but that's what she answered anyway. "I signed up right out of college. Seven years ago."

It didn't work. Caleb merely looked at her and said quietly, "I believe you know that is not what I meant."

She let out a long, compressed breath. He was going to demand it from her. And worse, she was going to give it to him. She couldn't seem to stop herself.

"Nine days."

He winced, closing his eyes and turning his head just slightly away, as if the answer had been worse than he'd been expecting. Yet he didn't change the subject, didn't try to gloss it over, and she knew he was not going to turn away from the ugly truth.

He muttered something that she barely heard, something in the dialect they used among themselves. It was close enough to the German that she could tell it was some kind of exclamation to God. And not a happy one. That her story had pushed him to that, oddly, took away some of the chill. She tried to respond in mock shock, to lighten things.

"Did you just—" she was going to say *swear,* but had the sudden thought that might be too serious an accusation to joke about, and changed course "—say something uncivil?"

"Sometimes it is beyond civilized men to remain civil."

She found this admission, and the anger that inspired it, somehow reassuring. The Amish pacifism had sometimes made her wonder if they truly felt anything; it had been one of the parents of the girls missing in Ohio that had told

her, with more patience that she likely had deserved at the time, that of course they felt anger
and all other normal human emotions. It was
how they channeled them, what they did about
them, that differed. It was not their way to flail
wildly, but to seek to understand God's will.

"You endured this for nine days."

His voice was stiff, as if he were keeping it
under strict control. It was somehow more po-
tent than an outburst of anger would have been.

"I was a bit more of a challenge to him than
those young girls."

"Yet you were little more than a girl yourself."

"I was a trained agent. And I had the profile
Quantico had done on him, so I knew a bit about
how to get to him."

She didn't explain how a couple of times, that
was the only thing that had kept her alive, playing on his need to torment, to break.

He'd never broken her. That was the one fact
that she'd clung to, the one thing that got her
through the nightmares and the flashbacks.

"It was two years ago," she began.

"And yesterday," he said, startling her again.

"Yes," she snapped.

The admission shattered the tentative wall she'd begun to rebuild in the warmth and golden glow of his home. The memories escaped again, and she knew she was far from over this episode.

"Yes," she repeated, too far gone now to care that her voice was trembling. The blanket had slipped away, yet the simple task of reaching for it seemed too much. She shouldn't be cold, not here in front of the stove, but she was, and she wrapped her arms around herself.

"Emma."

Caleb's voice had turned soft, had taken on an odd note she might have described as yearning in another man. She didn't dare describe it that way with him.

And then he moved, quickly. He swept her up out of the chair, grabbed the blanket in the same easy movement, wrapped it around her again. Then he lifted her in his arms—he was just as strong as she'd guessed he would be—and stunningly, with breath-stealing ease, sat down where she'd been, with her held tightly on his lap.

She shuddered, her mind battling a body that only now betrayed how much it had wanted this. She tried to pull back but instead nestled closer, the heat from him warming her as even the fire in the stove and Caleb's silly fan had failed to do. She simply couldn't make herself move, except closer. She wanted his warmth, his strength; it was why she'd come here, instead of running home to the ranch, or to Derek, or Tate, or even Gunnar, who perhaps would understand better than anyone.

His soothing heat reached where the fire had been unable to, down to her cold, quaking bones. She snuggled deeper, his arms held her, and gradually the shivering stopped.

She sighed.

This was an interesting feeling, she thought in some part of her brain the thaw had freed. It was as if the very house had wrapped itself around her, comforting, welcoming. But since

Caleb was the heart—and soul—of this home, that shouldn't be surprising.

What was surprising was that he had done this. Gone to such lengths to offer comfort. Again, what he'd done clashed with childhood memories of somber men with long, white beards. But she also remembered her father, a man who had held the respect and trust of the people of Paradise Ridge, standing on the Double C porch with a group of about five Amish men one sunny afternoon, all of them laughing uproariously over something.

She was suddenly seized with the desire to see Caleb laugh like that. He'd chuckled, had even laughed a couple of times on those evenings with the girls, but never had she seen him truly let out a big, male belly-deep laugh.

She glanced up at him, trying to imagine it. Right now he looked so odd she couldn't begin to. And as she looked at him, something shifted in his expression, his bright, clear eyes darkening. His head lowered slightly, and she saw his gaze shift to her mouth.

If it had been anyone but Caleb, she would have thought he was about to kiss her.

It was Caleb, and he was kissing her.

It was the briefest of touches, his lips over hers, yet a fire hotter than any the powerful little stove could produce seemed to spark instantly. As if this was the connection that completed a mega-watt circuit of the electricity his people shunned, something sharp, snapping and alive leaped between them.

And just as suddenly it was gone.

Caleb's sharp, jerking movement as he pulled back, the loss of warmth as he dropped his arms, the horror in his face as he stared at her, all made her feel as if she'd been dumped back out into the cold.

"No," he said, his voice nothing more than a harsh whisper. "Annie."

So it was true, she thought, her chest tightening against the admission of what she'd always sensed was true and what she'd been told often enough. He really had buried his heart with his dead wife.

Awkwardly he stood, holding her only so that she wouldn't fall when he did. He eased her down into the chair, gentle despite his obvious distress, and then backed away as if she had been the one to burn him.

"I should not have done that," he said stiffly. "I am not free to…"

Not free? "But she's…gone, Caleb."

It wasn't even for herself that she asked, she realized, even though this man had kindled something fierce and alive in her. It was for him, this man who was so vital, so strong and yet lived as if that part of life was over for him forever.

"Marriage," he said in that same strained voice, "is forever."

"Or until death," she said softly.

"No. Annie and I, we—"

He broke off, turning to face the woodstove as if he were the one freezing now.

As cold as the grave.

The phrase hit her like a sucker punch. They'd both felt it tonight, that kind of bone-deep, soul-sucking cold.

"You were happy," she said, her voice barely above a whisper. "She loved you."

"And I her. For seventeen years."

"Would she want this? Would she demand your heart be bound to her even into the grave?"

He spun around. Stared at her.

"I don't mean me," she said, her voice taking on an urgency as she tried to make that clear, even as her heart was saying, *Yes, you do.* "But someone, sometime… Surely she would want you to feel love again. Would want the girls to—"

"You have no knowledge and no right to speculate on what Annie would have wanted."

It was short, brusque, but to her surprise not angry. She would have expected anger from any other man. She wasn't sure the simple, calm statement of fact wasn't worse.

What she was sure of was that he was right. She should have kept out of it. And if the memory of that brief, searing kiss made the rest of her time here that much more awkward, then it was no more than she deserved. However much it taunted her, she knew one thing.

It would be even worse for Caleb.

Emma stood abruptly. She had to regain both her composure and her professionalism. But first, there was something else she had to do.

"Thank you," she said, thankful her voice sounded steady, unruffled, ruefully aware of how much effort achieving that tone had taken.

He flicked a glance at her. He opened his mouth as if to speak, then closed it again.

"I needed…comfort. And warmth. You gave it, without hesitation." And more, she thought, struggling not to let her emotions show any more than they already were. At least he had kissed her; had it been the other way around, she didn't think she'd be able to set it aside, even temporarily. She finished her statement somewhat formally. "That is what I thank you for."

His expression had changed as she spoke, as if he had momentarily forgotten the horror that had driven her here.

"You are welcome."

He said no more, made no reference to her personal nightmare, and for that she was grateful. In return she would let him off the hook for that kiss. She would never mention it and would do her best to forget it.

And even as she thought it, she knew her best would never, ever be enough to erase that kiss from her memory. Not when it had seared through her every defense, weakened though they'd been at the moment.

That was it, she told herself. Her defenses were up, but aimed in another direction, at that damned note. That was how he'd gotten under them so easily.

She crossed the few steps to the table where Caleb had set down the plastic evidence bag. She felt more confident now that she could look at it without falling apart. Caleb had given her that, had been the anchor that had kept her from spinning wildly out into space.

She picked up the envelope. She didn't have to read the words, with their wide, crayoned lines;

they were already etched into her mind. She focused instead on the writing itself.

The first thing she noticed was that it was different. The Monster had also used crayon, but had printed his notes in angular letters, with extreme pressure on the page. This was in cursive, in an entirely different hand. She noticed how the lines of the verse were so close together and tilted downward at the end, how the letters themselves got smaller toward the end of each line, making them hard to read in the wide crayon.

She was no graphologist, but she'd had some training and knew what generalities might apply here.

Cunning. Moody. Confused.

Not a good combination.

But also not the Monster.

She was steady now, her mind firing rapidly, no longer distracted by the possibilities and focusing on what was actually in front of her.

At her first glance, distracted as she was by the reappearance in her life of a note scrawled in crayon, the numbers had seemed to be a random string up and down each side of the note, in spots overlapping the lines of verse. Now she turned the paper sideways to look at them in their normal orientation. And realized it wasn't a continuous string; there was a gap. Two numbers, a gap, then five numbers.

On one edge, it seemed there was a small dot in that gap. A period? She looked at the other line of numbers, found nothing. But the tail of one of the letters intruded into that space; if there was a period, it could easily be hidden, written over. And was that a minus sign in front of one string?

It hit her then, suddenly, breath-stealingly.

GPS coordinates. Latitude, longitude.

She had a lead.

Chapter 21

The Poconos.

Emma stared at the map program on her phone.

She wasn't sure what it meant. Or, after the first leap of her pulse, even if it really was a lead. Someone had obviously left it for her, but why? Was it truly a lead or something intended to send her chasing off to some dead end?

Her gut said no. If that were the intention, they would have made it a bit more clear-cut, more obvious. This was cryptic and, except for the numbers, vague. If this was to throw her off, unless the person who scrawled this note was more clever than his writing indicated, it would have been more definite.

She studied the paper, her mind analyzing in the way she'd been unable to do when the first glimpse of it had blasted her composure into tiny shreds.

The numbers, concrete.

The verse, fractured, confused and…personal?

She couldn't pin down why she felt that way, but she couldn't deny her gut was saying the verse was more about the writer than the crime.

I must.

The repeated phrase echoed in her mind. And in her mind, she added the unwritten words that her gut told her fit.

I must. I don't want to, but I must.

Was this a cry for help? A plea to be stopped?

She could spend all night speculating on that and still be no closer to the truth, so she tried to focus on the facts of the matter. If she'd been given a specific location, as seemed clear, why? Was it truly a clue to the girls' location, or was it a trap?

It didn't really matter if it was meant as a trap. She had no choice but to follow the lead. She had nothing else after nearly a week of treading the same ground, pushing, prodding, asking.

The locals had done what they could, the officers assigned often covering the same ground she had, unfortunately with the same results. They'd taken to looking at her like some kind of miracle worker, expecting her to turn something up where they'd come up dry.

Or else they were glad to have a fed to blame, she'd thought wryly more than once.

The Poconos.

For hiding, it seemed both a logical and a dangerous choice. Logical because the mountains could offer concealment, yet dangerous because they were frequented by many thousands of visitors every year. While it was late in the year for fall color, cold for the lakes yet too early for the ski season, she supposed some people might like the brisk approach to winter in the mountains. Maybe gathering at family cabins for Thanksgiving in just a couple of weeks. That alone could markedly increase the population and the possibility of being discovered.

"You truly believe this is a clue?"

Caleb's quiet voice came from behind her.

"I believe it's as close to a possible clue as we've got," she answered. "It may be nothing, a prank, a coincidence…"

"Someone trying to frighten you?"

"There's the real coincidence," Emma said. "It just happened to be similar to the notes in the other case."

"You're certain of that?"

"The more I look at it, yes. The…Monster's notes were always in black crayon, on artist's paper and written in script that was almost calligraphy. We found out later he'd used crayon in case the note got wet, it wouldn't run. He was very…organized, precise. This—" she gestured with the bag "—has a very different feel."

"It looks as if a child had written it."

She gave him the best smile she could manage. "Exactly. This writing is completely different, childish, the paper torn out of a simple spiral notebook. It seems…hurried."

"Hurried?"

"As if he only had limited time. Or did it on impulse, before he could change his mind."

"You got all this from that scrap of paper?"

"You learn, after a while, to trust your instincts. You have them," she added, "because you recognized the childish appearance of it yourself. It's only a matter of training and experience to pick up the rest."

She saw a flash of something in his face before he lowered his gaze. On anything other than his work, she'd noticed he evidenced the typical Amish humbleness. Compliments did not hold the value they did in her world, not here where modesty was a hallmark. But she dared to hope he was also hiding that he was pleased at her words and that they had come from her.

"What happens now?" he asked, and she saw he was looking at the map on the glowing screen of her phone.

"This needs to be checked out," she said.

"You will call the police there?"

She'd thought of that, but now shook her head. "I'll call them, of course, but only for any information on the location. It's mostly rural, and this isn't something I'd want to send a small-town cop or county sheriff into cold. I'll call the Scranton FBI Resident agency. I think they're closest. Nothing against them, but this is already, as the saying goes, a federal case."

Caleb's brow furrowed. Sometimes she forgot that things—and sayings—that were common-place in her world had no place in his. And right now, she didn't want to take the time to explain.

"I'll go myself."

"Now? It is a long way. And dark."

"Probably at least a two-hour drive, according to this," she said, gesturing with the phone, still showing the map. "Maybe more at night, on some mountain roads. But it's the only thing that's turned up, and if it really is a clue to where the girls might be…"

Her voice trailed off, because anything else she might say didn't sound right. She couldn't admit she felt the need to redeem herself after her panicked reaction, after the way she'd run to Caleb for comfort, she who was supposedly the tough professional.

"You believe they might be here? At this place marked with those numbers?"

"Might," she stressed. "Those coordinates have to be there for a reason. I need to check it out."

"If the girls are there—"

"I'll bring Hannah home, Caleb. I promise."

She was all too aware that she hadn't said she'd bring her home safe or even alive. Then she saw in his face that she didn't have to. Caleb might be apart from the world she lived in, but he was not a fool. He knew perfectly well that the more time that passed, the less chance there was of Hannah returning home unharmed.

"I will go with you."

Startled, she gaped at him. That was the last thing she had expected to hear.

"What?" she asked, her voice sounding as wobbly as she suddenly felt at all that time alone with him and away from his restrictive life.

"Hannah and the others, if they are there, will

not trust you. They would be wary anyway, but now, after what they've been through, they will be terrified of any English."

The way her heart leaped at having a valid reason to say yes was a warning she knew she should heed. Taking this trip alone with him could lead to nothing but trouble for her.

"You can't. You have the girls."

"Mrs. Yoder will look after them. I will go next door and ask her."

He turned as if to go this instant.

"Wait," she said, her tone sounding more urgent than she liked, although what she was about to say was grim enough to warrant it. "Caleb, if they are there, it may not be...pleasant. They might even—"

"Be dead? Do you think I am not aware of that?"

It was as close to anger as she'd ever heard from him. It was echoed in his lean body, every line tight with it.

"I think that you've thought of little else for

three weeks," she said softly, taking the tension down a notch.

The anger seemed to drain from him. "Yes. And that is another reason I must come. I must know."

She made herself think logically. And logically, he had a point. If the girls were alive, they'd be frightened. If they'd been hurt, it would compound it. A familiar face would smooth the way greatly. She would just have to do her best to shield him from the worst, if that's what they found.

And she would have to keep herself in line, quash the silly way her mind went haywire and her body came to life merely in his presence. For the good of the case, for the good of Hannah Troyer and her friends, she was just going to have to compartmentalize, more strongly than she ever had before. She'd succeeded at most things she truly put her mind to, and she would succeed at this.

"Gather what you need," she instructed briskly.

"I'll make some calls. It'll be late when we get there, so I'll have to find a place we can stay."

She purposely made her voice as businesslike as possible, betraying no hint of what had gone through her mind at her own words about a place for them to stay and all those "we's" that had peppered her statement.

Caleb merely nodded. Within an hour Mrs. Yoder was settled in with sewing in her lap, sweetly helpful, and Caleb was coming downstairs with a small leather case that looked like a larger version of Derek's doctor's bag, not much bigger than her own go-bag. Obviously he was more than able to travel light. Or he was assuming they would be coming right back.

Or he simply didn't have the possessions that took up room. No electronics, obviously, not even an electric shaver—

Something struck her then. She knew the elders, particularly Deacon Stoltzfus, were distressed about Caleb's lack of beard. It went against their tradition that he'd shaved it, even in mourning. But they had indulged him, resisted anything more stern than warnings, had stopped short of any real punishment, such as shunning. It spoke of both his backbone and the respect and esteem in which he was held in his community.

Or of the love they all still held for the virtuous, perfect, departed Annie.

She felt a spark of bitterness shoot through her but had the grace to immediately chide herself for it. Being envious of a dead woman was a fool's path, and while she'd been doing—and thinking—a lot of foolish things lately, she wasn't that far gone.

Yet.

It was only then, when she again reminded herself she succeeded at most things she put her mind to, that she realized she was missing a crucial part of that success.

Those other times, she'd *wanted* to succeed.

Chapter 22

Caleb had to admit, if you had to travel, this electronic GPS system that talked to them as Emma drove was a convenience he could see the reason for.

But traveling, at least on a regular basis, any farther than it took to get to your work or visit family was exactly what their beliefs warned against. Too-easy travel led to more of it and thus put a strain on the bonds of the community. Not to mention it meant more time spent in the outside world. A certain amount was necessary and accepted, but it was not encouraged.

He realized, much too belatedly since they had already left both Paradise Ridge and Eden Falls miles behind them, that he probably should have informed one of the elders that he was going. Then he smiled inwardly. Mrs. Yoder would see to it that they had every detail she'd been able to glean first thing in the morning.

The girls would be surprised, but when she told them he'd gone to help find their aunt, he knew they would accept. Their own fear that they would never see the aunt who so adored them, and whom they adored in turn, had been growing every day, until even the voluble Ruthie had become quiet.

Except with Emma. In Emma's presence, all his girls, even shy, quiet Katie, seemed to blossom. Little Grace chattered endlessly at Emma, although her English was broken, made up of what she'd gleaned from her sisters since her own schooling, where English was taught, hadn't yet begun.

To her credit, Emma had begun to pick up the Pennsylvania Dutch language. She still slipped into German frequently, but she was learning quickly. When Katie had asked, she told them that she also spoke French and Spanish, and a smattering of Russian. Ruthie, being Ruthie, had demanded to know why, and Emma had explained that she had traveled a great deal with her parents, and her mother had made them all spend the long flights studying the country they were about to visit.

And that, Caleb thought, gave him what he needed. Nothing could have pounded home the great chasm between them more than that. His world, by its belief structure, was small and confined to itself. Hers literally was the globe, which she'd obviously traveled extensively. He would remember this, and it would be his shield against the crazy, unwanted thoughts he'd been having. It would allow him to sit in a vehicle with this woman who stirred him in ways he'd never known and keep his head about him.

At least, he'd thought it would. So far, he wasn't having much success.

He found himself watching her drive with a little too much interest. She did it with a casual ease, relaxed yet alert, showing no fear at striking off into the night. But why should she be afraid at something that would have terrified Annie and made he himself a little uneasy? She was, after all, of this world. And a trained law-enforcement professional on top of that. She could—and probably had—gone almost anywhere without fear.

Yet, she had been afraid tonight. She had been shaken to her very core; he was as certain of that as he was of his own name. It had been that fear that had driven him to do the unthinkable, to hold her, comfort her, draw her so close he could feel every line of her body, feel every shuddering breath she drew.

Now he suppressed a shudder at the memory of his own, unwelcome response to her. He didn't know which was worse, that he'd responded so to a woman who was clearly shattered at that moment or that he'd responded so to a woman who was not Annie.

But she was a woman who had sacrificed herself, subjected herself to horrors he could only begin to imagine but that she had known with grim clarity, for the sake of a stranger, a girl she didn't even know. Because it was her job?

He knew that wasn't the sole truth. He knew that it was because that was who she was. The kind of woman she was. And that told him more than he had even been able to process yet. The only word he'd been able to come up with was *heroic.*

And now here he was, rocketing through the darkness in a small, enclosed space with that very woman. Who not only was not Annie, but who was not like Annie in any way that he could see. She was brisk, businesslike, confident, almost sharp, not quiet, unassuming and shy like Annie.

Yet, she had been gentle and understanding with the girls, and they had come to like her so much so quickly it had startled him into studying her much more intently than he might have otherwise.

That, he thought more than a little ruefully, had been his downfall.

She was, however, very quiet now. She seemed

content simply to drive, not needing to talk. He thought he might rather she chatter, preferably about nothing much. And then he laughed at himself; it was hardly fair to think how unlike his quiet Annie she was and then turn around and complain because she was being quiet.

"Something funny?" she asked out of the darkness.

Either the laugh he'd thought was inward had slipped out, or she was that sensitive. He didn't think the former was true, and he couldn't discount the latter possibility; she was sensitive, to mood, to emotions, to things not said. He supposed it was necessary to her work, but it could be uncomfortable to someone who thought they were successfully hiding their own inner turmoil.

"My own stupidity," he muttered.

There was a moment of silence, and he stole a glance at her. Her face was faintly illuminated by the lights from the dashboard of the truck, and he was struck anew at how lovely she was.

"You are many things, Caleb Troyer," she said softly. "Stupid isn't anywhere on the list."

Something in her voice hit him hard, some undertone, a note that sounded impossibly like… longing?

"Emma," he breathed, forgetting in an instant the cultural gulf that spread between them, aware only that their physical distance was less than a yard.

"Is it just me, Caleb?" she asked, and this time he knew he hadn't mistaken the slight tremor in her voice. Nor could he find it in himself to deny what she was so clearly asking. Somehow pretending to misunderstand was not an option.

"No," he said, and even as he let out the admission, the impossibility of it flooded back.

"Thank you," she said, sounding relieved.

What he felt was anything but relief. Because now that he'd admitted it to her, he had to admit it to himself. He had never wanted this, had thought himself long past such feelings, had assumed they had died when Annie had slipped away from him.

Perhaps those feelings had, because what he was feeling for Emma was nothing like the quiet, steady love he'd had for Annie. That had been solid, reliable, unquestioned. Emma was fire and intensity, not at all quiet. But still, somehow he knew if she loved, it would be with the same kind of unshakable steadiness that had kept him and Annie together since childhood.

She had come when her brother had called, on her own time, at her own expense, simply because he was her brother. She'd never given up, treading the same ground over and over, hunting, searching, for the one thing that might give her a clue.

He had no doubt that kind of devotion and loyalty would extend to anyone she loved. An ache grew in him at the thought of her, someday, finding that love with a man of her world. He had no right to feel this way, yet he couldn't seem to help it. He'd wrestled with this for days now, probably longer beneath the surface. And his self-warnings, his prayers, his denial, none of it had done any good.

Desperate, he called on the only thing that came to mind that might put some distance between them. He remembered the little shock that had gone through him when, holding her, his fingers had brushed over the weapon she wore on her belt.

"Have you ever shot someone?"

She gave him a sideways glance that seemed almost startled, as he supposed the out-of-the-blue question deserved.

"That's a question I usually get from adolescent males."

Which is exactly what I'm feeling like now, he thought wryly.

"Are the Amish antigun?" she asked.

"No. We hunt, for food. But handguns…"

"Serve a purpose."

Yes, he thought. To kill other human beings.

"For me," she went on, "target practice mostly. Same with long guns. I could never hunt."

"Yet isn't that what you do? Hunt…people?"

"That's different. I couldn't hunt animals. If

they kill, it's simply what they are. It's their nature, and they can't change it. Men choose."

"To be animals?"

"Some, yes."

There was an odd undertone in her voice, more than just grim determination, but something that told him with no uncertainty that she would do whatever it took to protect those she loved.

And others. She would fight for him, he realized with a certainty he couldn't quite understand. And for his girls. She would fight to protect them all, if she had to, simply because that was who she was.

It was not his way, not the way of his people. God's will was God's will. But he was also aware enough to realize that, in some ways, it was people like her who made his way of life possible. If not for those who kept order on the outside, there could be no peace in his community. The kind of outsiders who saw them as weak, as easy targets, were kept in check by people like Emma.

It was a dilemma he'd been wrestling with

ever since she'd arrived in Paradise Ridge. He didn't question his faith, and yet something in the way she had sounded stirred him. So much that he had to speak words that grounded him, that brought him back to his life and faith.

"To hunt and kill men would go against everything I believe. I couldn't shoot a human being."

Even in the faint glow, he could see her fingers tighten around the steering wheel.

"That's all right," she said. "I can."

Chapter 23

There was a huge gap between them, Emma told herself as they drove on in silence. A gap too wide to be bridged? She didn't want to believe it, and yet this last conversation seemed to pound it home.

History and some horrific events had proven time and again the depths of Amish pacifist beliefs. But she was having an awful time trying to reconcile that with the urge to protect. If those girls had been hurt or worse…

She knew it was her own horrible ordeal that sometimes spiked her anger at this kind of predator to beyond containing. And it was those times, when she knew she was slipping out of control, that made her wonder if the help she needed, if what she'd been searching for, was not to be found in the office of yet another shrink, or counselor, or endless hard, physical workouts. Wondered if what she needed was what Caleb and his people had, that quiet acceptance that kept their lives, and seemingly their tempers, so peaceful and calm.

She flicked another sideways glance at him. He was facing straight ahead but looking downward, apparently at his hands in his lap. She saw, in the faint light, his profile. Strong chin, sculpted nose, classically handsome lines. All softened by the impossibly long sweep of his lowered lashes, a darker semicircle against his cheek in the faint light.

In that moment she admitted at last what she'd been fighting since the first moment she'd caught a glimpse of him and her knees had gone wobbly.

She wanted this man. As crazy, as impossible as it was, he sent her pulse racing, heating her body in ways she'd never experienced before.

What had happened tonight had only intensified her reaction. He'd held her, comforted her in a way she'd never known—in fact would never have allowed—from any other man. His warm, steady strength had warmed her, had taken the turmoil from her, calmed her in a way she wouldn't have thought possible before him.

Oh, yes, she wanted him.

And she couldn't have him.

She knew that, knew it as surely as she knew anything. She couldn't have him, the gap truly was too wide, and the sooner she stopped thinking about it, the better.

Is it just me, Caleb?

No.

That simple exchange slammed through her mind like a careening mountain sled. It slowed her brain so that she almost didn't react to the announcement from the GPS that they were at their destination.

The small, tidy cluster of resort cabins had come on a recommendation from Derek, who had once taken his wife there in an effort to soothe her troubled spirit. It had bought him some time, but Tess's instability was too deep, and two years ago Derek's life had been shattered by her death. But he seemed to have come to terms with it since and said the place would serve Emma's needs nicely.

The proprietor, a jovial retiree from New Jersey, met the late arrival with a smile. Mr. Rinaldi remembered Derek—few who met him did not—and if he was surprised at her appearance, it didn't show. He seemed much more than willing to talk and excited to have an FBI agent staying there, but after a few questions, she realized he wasn't going to be any help. In fact, he'd probably have the news of the federal agent staying in one of his cabins all over the mountains soon, she thought as she glanced back to see him picking up the phone with an animated smile on his face.

But she had the key and directions to the last cabin in the row, closest to the small lake or large pond, depending on your advertising spin. Lucky for her, the man had said, that it wasn't high season, when he was usually full. He'd opened the cabin up, made sure it was clean and stocked, and turned the heat on, so she was good to go.

Caleb had stayed in the car, perhaps beyond explaining his presence here to someone even more of an outsider to him than she was.

The building she stopped in front of was small, but well kept and solid-looking, at least as far as she could see in the dark. It appeared to be a story and a half, and had been described as a one bedroom with a sleeping loft.

There was a small covered porch at one end, with a welcoming light. She grabbed her go-bag and her kit and started that way, key in hand, hyperaware that Caleb had silently exited the vehicle and was behind her. She saw the cabin had a row of windows along the side facing the water, and it nestled among tall evergreens and large boulders strewn in an artful arrangement only Mother Nature could manage. In pleasanter times, she could imagine a family using the picnic table that sat outside, as her own family had often done at home during long-ago summers.

When they'd been whole.

Emma blinked away the sting of tears at the sharp jab of memory. She tried to get the key in the lock, but her vision was blurry.

"Are you all right?"

Did the man never miss anything? And how many times had he asked her that? But his voice was so quiet, so gentle, she found herself speaking of what she rarely spoke of anymore.

"I used to think it would stop, that someday I'd be able to envision my family without tearing up over how it has changed."

The key caught, but a tremor in her hand sent it scraping sideways and she had to try again.

"Many more were wounded that day than were in those planes and buildings," Caleb said.

"Yes. And the wounds never really heal. I've come to accept it will always ache. "

"Should you feel nothing, as if they had never lived?"

"Of course not. I just thought…life goes on, and as it got more distant…"

She still couldn't get the damned key in the lock.

"My people have struggled with this greatly. The idea of killing for your God is…anathema to us. The worst possible betrayal of who God is and His intent."

"On that," she said, "we are in complete agreement."

She tried with the key once more. Only this time, Caleb reached out and put his hand over hers to steady it. The moment his fingers brushed over the back of her hand, a different emotion exploded in her. It was no more welcome than the remembered grief, but at the moment, it was also much more powerful.

Heat shot through her, and she knew it wasn't her imagination that his hand was lingering over hers. For a span of time that seemed endless, they stood there, scarcely breathing, his hand over hers. She felt as if they'd tapped into a current that only needed a touch to complete its circuit and begin to hum between them.

She had to move, to do something, get the door

open and get inside before she did something impossibly foolish. And she had to quash the rebellious, reckless part of her brain that was saying, *He kissed you, didn't he? Your turn.*

The key slid home, the door opened, and she wasn't sure which of them had turned the knob. She needed to find the light switch, not trusting herself to be alone in the dark with him here in this place where neither her world nor his could intrude.

She set her bags on the table she could barely make out next to the door. She unclipped her holster from her belt and laid the weapon beside them. Then she turned to look beside the doorway in the logical place for a light switch.

And found herself barely an inch away from Caleb, who had stepped in after her and closed the door.

"Emma," he said, sounding as breathless as she felt.

And then, against all her own warnings, she listened to that little internal voice.

She kissed him.

She had to stretch up slightly, at her height enough of a novelty to be appreciated. She thought he might recoil, he'd been so churned up by his own actions when she'd come to him, but he didn't. For a moment he went stock-still, doing nothing as she leaned into him and pressed her lips to his. She knew it was wrong, knew she shouldn't, but she couldn't stop herself. She had to know if it had been a fluke, an accident of timing, a result of her chewed-up emotions, that fierce heat that had erupted in her before.

And then he was kissing her back, his arms coming around her, his mouth no longer resisting but participating, and she had her answer. It had been no fluke, no accident. The fire was there, as raging as if it had been building beneath the surface ever since that first, slight kiss.

She was barely aware of moving, yet somehow they'd found the sofa in front of the fireplace at the end of the main room of the cabin. She sank down, unable to stand as the heat consumed her. Some sane part of her mind thought he would pull away, but he went with her, pressing her back against the cushions, deepening the kiss as if it had been his idea in the first place.

She gasped at the feel of his weight on her, the feel of his long, leanly muscled body against her, chest to toe. She wondered, in that last moment of sanity, if he was as stunned as she that it could leap to life so fast, so hot, so deep.

And in that shrinking part of her mind that was still functioning, she felt a spurt of purely feminine pleasure that she had been able to push Caleb, strong, quiet, always-in-control Caleb, to this. She wasn't particularly proud of the thought, but neither would she deny the power of it.

She ran her hands over as much of him as she could reach, felt trails of heat tracking over her body as he did the same to her. On and on it went, spiraling higher with every stroke, every caress. And she delighted in the obvious fact that he was with her, holding, touching, caressing, and continuing a kiss so deep and so hot that she wished the need to breathe could be suspended so it could never end.

But it did have to, if only so she could nibble her way down the strong, masculine cord of his neck to the hollow of his throat, glad there was no shirt collar to get in her way.

"Emma," he whispered, his voice low, husky and almost gasping, which only threw more fuel on the fire already nearly out of control. Through the rising haze of pleasure, she was aware that she'd been a little afraid that if he spoke, it would be the name of his dead wife. That it was not, that it was her name, telling her he was completely aware of who he held, whose body he was driving to the point of insanity.

She couldn't get close enough, couldn't hold him close enough; she wanted the barriers of clothing out of the way. She could feel how aroused he was, and when he pressed her harder against him, the flames leaped even higher.

One of his hands slipped upward from her waist and cupped her breast. Her rapid breathing came to a shocked halt as she held it, in an agony of tension, waiting, afraid to move even as her stomach clenched and her nipple tightened in anticipation.

When his fingertips brushed over that eager flesh, she gasped aloud. Her back arched upward almost involuntarily; more, she wanted more. Needed more. Needed more than she could ever remember needing in her life.

Caleb's low, guttural groan only fired that need.

She barely recognized this creature, spared a split second for the irony of it being this man who turned her into this wild, desperate, aching female, with her destined mate so close and yet so far.

Destiny, apparently, had a wicked sense of humor.

But the knowledge couldn't stop this rising tide of heat and need. She wasn't sure anything could. It would take a strength greater than she had, she knew that.

It would take a strength like Caleb's. And somewhere, obviously, he'd found it.

He stopped. He went still for a long, strained moment. Then he shifted off her.

"I cannot do this."

His voice was so strained, so harsh she could almost feel the turmoil in him. Or maybe it was her own she was feeling.

"Caleb," she began, but stopped, with no idea what to say.

"I want this too much. These feelings are too much. *You* are too much. I cannot." He drew in a shuddering breath. "They are right," he muttered. "Leaving the community leads to forgetting it."

He moved as if to rise, and she grasped his shoulder. "Please, don't."

"I—"

"We'll stop. Just...don't leave."

Because I'll die if you do. I'll freeze to death if I don't have your heat. I'll become a quivering mess without your strength.

"You ask much of me."

"Yes." There didn't seem any point in denying it. "Because you are strong enough."

After a long, silent moment during which she could sense his inner battle, he sank back down beside her on the big couch. She didn't mind that it was rather lumpy beneath her, was glad that it was big enough to hold them both yet narrow enough that they had to be in intimate contact.

"Caleb," she began again.

"Please. Do not. It is best we don't speak of this."

She gave in, thinking that as chaotic as her own feelings were, they probably didn't hold a candle to his.

"For now," she agreed, knowing that not talking about it, not facing this now wasn't going to make it go away.

And thinking that he was likely right, what they had to talk about was better done in the light of day rather than the tempting darkness.

She would have sworn the last thing she was likely to do was drift off to sleep, and yet she did. Not only did she sleep, but after the heat and emotion had finally ebbed, she slept soundly, waking only once to listen to Caleb's steady

breathing and realize with a little jolt of pleasure that in sleep he'd again wrapped his arms
around her. She snuggled into his warmth and
slipped back into the most peaceful sleep she
could remember in ages.

Hours later, the sharp, shattering sound of broken glass jolted her awake.

Chapter 24

For an instant Emma was confused, disoriented and distracted by Caleb, who was already beginning to sit up.

"Was that glass?" he asked.

Another time, she would love to tease him about that sleepy voice, another time she would ponder the wonder of waking up with him. But the agent within her had awakened, too, and she scrambled to her feet. Automatically she checked the time; just before dawn.

The broken window was easy to see, about halfway along the wall that faced the water. Shards of glass glinted on the floor in the moonlight streaming through. And a foot farther into the room lay…something.

Emma didn't stop now, glanced only long enough to make a guess at trajectory on the object.

"Don't touch anything," she said as she skirted the broken glass, racing toward the door. She grabbed up her Glock from the table as she went, shucking the holster heedlessly.

She inched the door open and for a moment just stood there listening. She heard nothing in the still night, only the faint rustle of high boughs in the trees as a slight breeze wafted above.

She stepped outside, weapon at the ready as she went, keeping to the shadow of the building until she reached the broken window. She looked in the direction she guessed the rock must have come from. Again she paused, listening, barely breathing.

Nothing.

Whoever had thrown that rock was long gone,

her senses and her instincts told her. She went back to the cabin.

Caleb was standing just inside the door. She couldn't see his face clearly, but tension was evident in his posture. She didn't have time to deal now; she needed to look at what had been thrown through the window.

Thankfully, he didn't speak. Glad this time that he tended toward taciturnity, Emma got to work.

She walked quickly over to the broken glass, and Caleb followed. She knelt to examine the baseball-size object. "I should have turned on the light," she muttered, almost to herself. Then, normally and aimed at Caleb, she added, "Could you get the switch?"

He hesitated just long enough for her to realize he might not have any idea where switches were traditionally put.

"There should be one by the door, so you can get it right when you come in."

Without a word he walked in that direction, and after a moment, she heard a faint click. She blinked at the sudden flood of light from an overhead fixture, but she never took her eyes off the object that had come through the window.

That it was a rock was obvious. Large and heavy enough so that it wouldn't take a tremendous amount of force for it to break the glass, yet small enough to be easily thrown. What was wrapped around it, secured by two loops of a twisted rubber band, wasn't so obvious.

It appeared to be fabric of some kind. A dark blue, plain, no pattern.

She rose and crossed the room to get her kit. She opened the small aluminum case and quickly took out several things, then donned a pair of latex gloves she took from the box in a back corner of the case. Then she unfolded a sheet of plastic onto the floor next to the rock.

A few moments later, it was all spread out before her. The rubber band was the ubiquitous tan of millions used in offices across the country. The rock was odder, very black and rough, except for one completely flat side. The edges around that side were sharp, uneroded. And there were bits of what looked like mortar or cement on the flat side, as if it had been part of something larger. But she would start with one thing that was unique, that scrap of blue fabric.

She flattened it out as best she could. It was stained, one spot round and brownish like dried mud, the other darker and irregular.

She sensed rather than saw Caleb crouch beside her, sensed he was staring at the three things laid out there.

"Hannah," he breathed.

She flicked a glance at him. "What?"

He indicated the cloth with a rather sharp nod of his head. "That cloth...she was wearing a dress of that cloth. That day."

She looked at him full-on then. "This cloth? Or at least, cloth like this?"

He nodded.

"Is it unusual?"

"It is...bright."

Emma looked back at the fabric. It didn't look bright to her. It was a deep, dark royal blue. A very nice color, actually, she thought. She supposed that next to the blacks and grays that were more typical of his community, it might seem bright.

"Hannah has…a weakness for such things. She loves making clothes for herself, for the girls."

"She's good at it?" Emma struggled to sew on a button, usually ending up with bloodshed.

"She is an accomplished seamstress. But she is always pushing the boundaries."

"And this—" Emma gestured at the blue cloth "—is pushing the boundaries?"

"Yes. It is not plain."

She tried to visualize a dress of this color among the drabber backdrop of the women she'd seen so much of in the past ten days. And had to admit it would stand out. Which would push the boundaries, as Caleb had said.

"Did she get in trouble for it?"

"She was not warned, not officially. But…disapproval was expressed."

"And how did she handle that?"

"She always chafed under the restrictions.

Other things she accepted without complaint. But the dress..."

"Maybe she should make clothes for outsiders."

"She has thought of it, I believe. She has always drawn pictures, and once she was caught with a magazine full of English clothing."

A fashion magazine, Emma guessed as she turned her attention back to the cloth.

She didn't explain what she was doing as she tested the stains, taking care to disturb everything as little as possible, so that the lab could get more detailed results from a full gamut of tests if necessary.

But there was one test she needed to do right here and now. Moments later she was staring at the cotton swab giving her the grim truth.

Blood.

"Well, damn it all."

Emma nearly jumped at the sound of the voice from outside. She took a few seconds to secure the swab, then picked up her sidearm, rose and stepped to the broken window.

There stood Mr. Rinaldi, staring up at the damage with a frown. When he saw Emma at the window, he called out to her.

"You all right?"

"Yes."

"Wife told me she heard breaking glass. I thought she'd been dreaming, but she nagged at me until I had to get up and take a look." His expression turned glum. "Guess I'm gonna have to tell her she was right."

He looked almost more upset about that than the damage, Emma thought.

"I better come in and take a look, get it cleaned up for you."

To her surprise, the man didn't seem at all startled to see Caleb.

"Figured a pretty girl like you wouldn't be alone," he said with a smile that took any snark out of the comment. Then, to Caleb, he gave a male-to-male wink. "You're a lucky young man."

Emma opened her mouth to explain, to deny

the assumptions he was making, but Caleb spoke first, startling her.

"I have not been called that in a long time."

He said it quietly, musingly, as if he were having trouble comprehending.

"Well, that's odd," Mr. Rinaldi said.

Emma shifted her attention back to the older man. He was staring at the rock.

"What's odd?" she asked.

"That rock. Looks like that stuff old man Carter used to build that fancy fire pit of his. He's a little off center, you know. Wanted it to look like a volcano or something, like they got in Hawaii."

"Lava rock?"

"Yeah, that's the stuff. I mean, it's not really— he was too cheap to pay to get the real thing. He got some outfit over in Philly to color up some concrete and make 'em."

"Who is this Carter?"

"Was."

"Was?"

"He died a few years back. He left the place to

his grandkids, but they moved to Jersey, don't get up here anymore."

"So it's…empty?"

"Yeah. They'd sell it, I think, but with the way things are…" He shrugged. "Plus, it's kinda off the beaten path, if you know what I mean. Out there a ways."

"Isolated?"

"Yeah. Too much for most people."

But perfect for hiding what you were doing.

"Can you give me directions?"

"Sure. You going out there?"

"Yes."

"Good. If you find who did this, tell 'em they owe me for a window."

Emma didn't tell him that if she found whoever had thrown that rock, a window would be the least of the things they'd be paying for.

Chapter 25

Caleb was at the car before she gathered up her gear and got there.

"Maybe you should—"

"You think Hannah and the others may be there," he said.

He obviously hadn't missed a thing in there, had followed her thought process perfectly. He also obviously wasn't about to listen to any suggestion that he stay here and wait for her to check it out.

"Maybe."

"That test you did, on the cloth. It was for blood, wasn't it."

It wasn't really a question, and she gave him a

sidelong as she tacitly gave in to his insistence on going and got into the truck.

"I am not of your world, but I am not ignorant of it," he said, interpreting the look accurately.

She pulled out her phone and checked for a signal. It was weak, only one bar, and she was glad she'd called the resident office last night, although they'd said no one could get out here until noon. Then the bar vanished, and when she tried to call Tate, it wouldn't go through. So she sat for a moment, typing in a text message explaining she had a solid lead and including the lengthy directions. The place apparently had no address to enter into the GPS, and since they had no exact coordinates, she had to just do the best she could. In case anything happened, she wanted some record somewhere of where she—they—had gone.

The sun was fully up now, which made following the rather lengthy directions a little easier. As was often the case in the country, the directions were by landmark—a certain tree, a bridge over a creek, even a frog-shaped rock. There was no "turn right at the convenience store" out here.

But Caleb proved a more than able navigator, always warning her of the next course change enough in advance that they only had to back-track once, when she overshot the entrance to the rough gravel road that was their last turn. But now they were on their way again.

"Last night," he began.

Her stomach knotted as she negotiated a par-ticularly rough patch. She didn't know what to say about last night. It had been simultaneously the sweetest, hottest and most painful night of her life. Having him so close and yet not being able to—

"You went outside, not knowing what—or who—was out there."

Well, that blew a hole in my sails, she thought, realizing he hadn't been thinking of those heated moments at all.

"It's my job," she said, trying to keep her voice level.

"A terrible job."

"A necessary job."

"In your world."

She glanced at him. "And occasionally in yours."

"Only when your world seeps over into ours."

"Claiming perfection?"

"No. Only striving for it. It is the best man can do, to continually strive."

"Caleb," she began, then hesitated, not sure what she wanted to say, and ended finally with a simple, "I'm sorry."

"I am sorry you must do such a job. You are very brave."

"I'm trained."

"Are the two mutually exclusive?"

She shot him a longer glance that time, as long as she dared on that road. Was he actually making a joke?

She caught the faintest twitch at one corner of his mouth. And she couldn't stop the grin that spread across her face. She'd love to spend the rest of her life making sure that happened more often. That his devastating smile appeared more often. That his wonderful laugh echoed in her ears—

She stopped her own thoughts dead in their tracks. That way lay more than folly; that way lay insanity. Yet when she stole another glance at him, she could have sworn she saw her own inner turmoil reflected in his face, in his eyes.

Is it just me, Caleb?

No.

For a moment he looked away. But then he turned back, and this time it was all there, in his face, in his eyes, unmasked, open for her to see.

She nearly forgot she was driving and had to wrench the wheel to get them back on the gravel and keep them out of the drainage ditch that ran beside the road that had now become little more than a rocky dirt track.

She didn't dare look at him again after that. It had to have been a conscious decision to let her see that, to let her see that he was feeling everything that she was feeling. But knowing that didn't make any difference, didn't make things any less impossible.

Because it was impossible.

Wasn't it?

Caleb would never leave his world for hers. And she couldn't blame him for that.

That little voice she so often relied on chose that moment to pipe up and say, as if it were the most obvious thing, *But you could leave yours.*

There it was. The thought she'd been denying had even been in her mind for days now. The thought that should be ridiculous, should be patently absurd.

And yet…

She forced herself to watch the road, which had gotten even narrower. It seemed to wind on and on, and soon *remote* didn't seem a strong enough word for it. Mr. Rinaldi had said it was about three miles back in, give or take, and she was about to decide his assessment had been off by quite a bit when Caleb spoke.

"There it is."

She glanced at him, saw he was looking ahead to the left. It was up ahead enough and so far back in the trees it took her a moment to see the straight lines of the roof on the building painted the same green as the trees. She guessed he was right, since it was the only building they'd seen for the past mile and the distance was about right based on Mr. Rinaldi's directions.

"Foolish," Caleb said.

"What?"

"The solar panels on his roof."

She'd noticed, wondered if that was what Mr. Rinaldi had meant when he'd said "old man Carter" was a bit of a nut.

"What about them?"

"He would not get enough sun where he has them. The trees are too thick. A cleared space to the west or south would be better."

She nearly gaped at him. "You know about solar panels?"

"I have a cousin who is beginning a business of building them. Many Amish communities are exploring the possibilities."

"Electricity from solar power?"

"It is not electricity itself we avoid. It is being connected to the world that would provide it in the conventional way. Solar would make us more independent than relying on gas for our generators, to power our refrigerators and stoves."

It made sense, she supposed. In an Amish sort of way.

She couldn't deny their ingenuity. And she was finding their simple lives more and more appealing every day. Just as she understood more and more about why they kept themselves apart.

Just as her attraction to this man grew more powerful every day. Powerful enough that she was actually, in a serious way, thinking about abandoning everything she knew, everything she'd grown up with and lived with as an adult. If she'd been a teenager, her mother would have cautioned her about changing who she was for a boy. But she was an adult, and on some inner level she knew that she had already changed, that her work had changed her, that what she'd been through two years ago had changed her, in ways that were deep and permanent.

But, she told herself sternly now, if she wanted to be around to ponder that change, to make the huge decisions facing her, she'd better pay attention to the here and now of her current world.

She found a wider spot in the narrow road and pulled the truck over. They were about a hundred feet away from the cabin, which was now almost invisible through the thick trees.

Emma turned off the truck. Automatically she checked her sidearm, verifying it was secure but moved freely in the holster. She rolled down the window partway so she could listen for any sounds from the cabin. She heard nothing.

She could almost feel Caleb's gaze on her. She turned to look at him.

"Stay here. I'm going to go take a look."

"But it is my—"

"Please, Caleb. Stay here. I can't be distracted."

"Distracted?"

"Yes. And I would be. I can't do my job properly if I'm too worried about you."

"You do not need to worry—"

"Let's not talk about what I need," she said pointedly enough that he flushed. "Last night may have meant nothing to you—"

"No." This time he interrupted her. "It did not mean nothing."

He lowered his gaze. She looked at him, at the thick sweep of his lashes, dark against his cheeks. "It meant too much," he said, his voice a low, rough whisper that sent a shiver up her spine as if he'd touched her.

And she couldn't deny the feeling she had that in that moment, with his reluctant admission, her life had just changed, irrevocably and forever.

Chapter 26

For a long moment Emma just sat there looking at him. And then he lifted his gaze to her face. And what she saw there both thrilled and frightened her.

"What are we going to do?" The whispered question broke from her before she could stop it.

"This is…impossible," he said.

"Yes. And yet," she said shakily.

"And yet," he repeated. "I have not felt this… wanting before. I wish to be with you all the time. It is so powerful that I fear it will consume me."

As bald admissions of want went, this one was pretty impressive, Emma thought, trying to fight down the whirl of feelings his words had roused in her.

"I know. I feel it, too," she said, wondering if she was doing this, admitting all this, because she really thought something might go wrong up there. True, she was on her own, without backup, but she was trained and fairly skilled with a handgun.

She should be focusing on her job, not the fact that she had fallen like a stack of his lumber for a man who, even though he'd admitted he felt the same, might never be hers.

"I wish," Caleb said, his voice almost a broken thing, "that there was a way."

"Yes," Emma said, thinking she could live on that wish, if she had to. "And I want nothing more than to stay right here and hash this out, fight through all the barriers between us, until we find some way to be together. But this must come first."

"I will come and—"

"Caleb, please. Worrying about you, where you are, if you're safe, could get me killed."

He went a little pale. Perversely, she felt another little thrill at this instant sign of worry.

"I only meant to come partway. In case you needed help. And if someone runs…"

She drew back a little. "But you don't fight."

"No. I will not. But I do not think in this case simply stopping an escape would be frowned on. And if it is, so be it."

She had a feeling she didn't yet fully understand the size of that decision. But she couldn't waste any more time thinking about it or talking about it.

"They may be armed," she warned.

"I am determined, but not a fool."

"There's a rifle in the back of the truck," she began.

Something flashed across his face, a weary sadness that tore at her. "I would never use it on another human being."

"I know that," she said. "But they don't."

He blinked. And then, looking as if it were almost in spite of himself, one corner of his mouth lifted.

"And," she added, "seeing you armed just might stop them from shooting at you."

"I will carry it," he agreed, "as long as we're understood."

"We are," Emma said softly.

Again his expression shifted. And Emma told herself she was reading too much into it, that he couldn't really feel the same little jolt of pleasure mixed with fear at the simple use of the word *we*. She desperately wanted there to be a "we" but feared the gulf between them, between their lives, was too wide.

"Come, then. We'll find a place for you to wait and watch. Don't slam the door."

Only you, she thought, *could end up hundreds of miles from home, working on a kidnapping case that isn't even in your jurisdiction, with your only backup a committed pacifist you just happen to be in love with, from a religious community that would likely try and stop you two from ever being together.*

If her mission wasn't so serious, she'd laugh at herself.

They worked their way through the trees as silently as possible. For a big man, Caleb was light on his feet and seemed to know how to move through the woods making little noise. He carried the rifle easily, familiarly.

Their conversation about hunting animals versus men ran through her head again. Were they too far apart? Could the gap between them never be bridged, no matter their feelings for each other?

As she made her way toward the cabin, fearing what she might find, the idea grew in her mind. The idea of leaving all this, of never again having to look upon man's depravity and cruelty, of not having to face evil day after day after evil day, was growing almost too appealing to resist.

And the idea of having Caleb to comfort her when the nightmares came was enough to put it over the top.

With one of the greatest efforts she'd ever had to make, she put it all out of her mind to focus on the job. When they reached a thin spot in the trees where there was a partial view of the cabin, she whispered to him to stay here and made him promise that he would. She didn't worry about it after that; he'd given his word, and Caleb Troyer would keep it. She had absolutely no doubts about that, and her last unprofessional thought before she put on the mental armor she needed was that there were few people outside her family she could say that about.

She turned her back on him. She couldn't concentrate on what she had to do otherwise. She worked her way as silently as possible through the trees, paralleling but not taking the clear path that led to the cabin. This was a very different countryside than the flatland and gentle rises of home, but she'd trekked through some tougher places in her career, and she arrived at the cabin quickly.

And once more she paused, watching, listening, for any sign of life. Leaves, pine needles and other debris had piled up here and there, yet the path was clear. Her heart rate kicked up when she saw what looked like drag marks along the softer edge of the hardened dirt path.

But there wasn't a sign of anyone around. No vehicle parked in the open carport or anywhere else close by. No sound came from the cabin. Still, she drew her weapon as she approached.

She made a full circuit, stopping only when she came to the small patio on the back side of the building. In the middle was the fire pit Mr. Rinaldi had mentioned. And it did indeed match the rock that had been hurled through the window at dawn.

She didn't bother to check for any spots that looked as if they were missing a rock the right size, since she was fairly sure there wasn't another pit like it close by. The shiny, sharp-edged black rock seemed jarringly out of place.

She rounded the patio and saw that there was a door on that end of the cabin.

It was open.

Her pulse kicked up a notch, but her training kicked in, and she conducted her search in a methodical, precise way Tate would have been proud of. It didn't take long; the cabin was small, without even enclosed closets.

Nothing. Not even a stray fast-food wrapper or water bottle.

Had this been a wild-goose chase?

She exited the cabin via the same door, near the garish fire pit. She noticed then a pile of what was apparently leftover stones, over by a shed half-hidden by a big tree.

A fairly large shed.

Back on alert, she went that way. There was no window in the shed, so she paused with her ear to the door. Nothing.

There was a padlock on the door, and it was shiny and new compared to most everything else here. That alone sparked suspicion. But a lock was only as strong as what it was fastened to, and this door looked as if a good breeze would take it down.

As it turned out, it took only a good, solid foot plant near the hasp; the screws pulled right out of the rotting wood. The door swung open, then stopped as it hit something inside. She pushed and it moved a little, but not much. Another shove got it open enough that she could slide in.

And then wished she hadn't.

She'd seen other sights like this, many bloodier and more gruesome, but this one seemed worse somehow. And the morning light streaming through the partially opened door made it seem even worse.

She'd found two of the missing girls.

Chapter 27

Emma tried to stop Caleb, when he'd heard the noise of the breaking door and come running. But he pushed past her with a strength and determination she couldn't match without taking action that might injure him, and she couldn't bring herself to do that. Besides, she told herself, striving desperately for a shred of professionalism, he would be able to tell her if these two tragically young women were indeed who she thought they were.

Caleb made a sound low in his throat. The two women—girls, really—lay sprawled on the dirt floor, their hands bound behind them, their dead eyes open and staring. He staggered backward. Emma caught him, eased him around to lean against the shed wall, his back to the horror within.

"Hannah isn't—"

She broke off, wondering if she was somehow wrong. True, she'd done only a quick visual check, but neither of the two broken, tragic women matched Hannah's description.

"No." Caleb confirmed it, his voice flat, hollow.

"Miriam?" she asked. "And Rebecca?"

"Yes."

"Then Hannah may well still be alive."

He didn't seem to react at all.

"Caleb, she's not here, not in the house. There's a decent chance she—"

"Decent? What is there that is decent in your world?"

"Caleb—"

"Your world is decadent, brutal and ruthless."

His voice was cold, harsher than she'd ever heard from him. She'd seen this before, in the families of victims. Caleb might not be a blood relative of these two women, but in his heart and mind they were his sisters just as Hannah was.

"It can be, yes," she said, seeing no point in arguing the obvious.

"It has stolen the lives of two girls more innocent and pure than any seen in that world. How can you be a part of it?"

"I'm beginning to wonder that myself."

The truth escaped her before she could stop it, and once it was out she stubbornly refused to wish she could call it back. She finally faced the fact that something had changed in her. The constant exposure to the quiet, simple life she'd experienced the past few days seemed to have seeped into her bones somehow, making this return to the reality of her life and work more jarring than anything she'd ever experienced.

Then there was Caleb. Caleb with his pure, solid goodness, with the quick mind and the skilled hands, who produced items of such simple beauty and took such care of his three daughters.

Caleb, who right now leaned against that wall,

his head bowed, refusing to look at anything, especially her. Gone was the easy warmth that had burgeoned between them. Gone was the heat that had followed and the heady sense of wonder at what they'd found in the darkness of the little cabin. Caleb was shutting down, as if this reminder of the world she lived in proved she could never live in his.

Emma went through the motions of what came next: calling local authorities to the scene, overseeing the processing of that scene as best she could without stepping on local toes and most of all warning them all of the need to be vigilant for any other evidence. Hannah was still out there somewhere, and anything they found here might be the difference between finding her alive and a third death added to the ugly total.

It was late by the time the scene was processed and she had all information she could glean from the locals.

"You'll send the evidence and autopsy reports ASAP?" she asked the lieutenant who had come out to oversee the scene. He seemed very young

to her, but he'd been military and handled everything with a promising efficiency. Not to mention that he had a little less wariness of the feds,
given he'd sort of been one himself as an investigator in the MPs.

"I'll see you get everything as soon as it's completed, Agent. And you'll let me know if indeed
this is connected to your other case in Ohio?"

"I will."

It had been a long day, and it occurred to
Emma that staying overnight and starting back
in the morning might be easier. But one look at
Caleb's stiff, closed expression warned her that
was a suggestion that would not be met with any
agreement.

Given what had happened between them last
night, he was probably right. Although judging
by the rigid expression and the stiff lines of his
body, he had less than no interest in ever being
alone with her again. As if somehow this was
all her fault.

It wasn't fair, but then, life wasn't fair. Hadn't
she learned that early on, when her parents, two

of the best people to ever walk the planet, were taken out in a senseless, outrageous attack on innocents?

It was a long, silent drive back from the mountains. She finally broke the silence as they neared the edge of Paradise Ridge.

"I'll take Mrs. Yoder home so she doesn't have to walk in the dark."

"I will walk her home."

"Then I should stay with the girls while—"

"No." Caleb's voice was so flat, so adamant it was all she could do not to physically recoil. "There has been enough of your world intruding here today."

Emma couldn't help but be stung by what appeared to be his determination to keep her from seeing his daughters at all. She told herself she was reading too much into it, that he was reacting to the horror they'd found, and coupled with the tenuous hope that Hannah wasn't somewhere else they hadn't found yet, in the same condition as those girls, he had simply shut down.

And shut her out. Coldly and completely. He'd

clearly expressed he had a great distaste for her world and no interest in having her in his.

When he got out of the truck, he walked into the house and never even looked back.

She drove on, the truck seeming very empty. The light of day faded, dying away just as her silly dreams were.

It was dark once again when she pulled through the gates of the Double C. But the lights were on at the main house, welcoming her home.

Home.

This was her home and always would be. And all the stolen moments she'd spent imagining creating a home with Caleb—imagining living the kind of quiet, peaceful life he led, the kind of life that had become more and more appealing to her the longer she spent dealing with the ugly cruelty of her own world—had been no more than a fool's dream.

It was ironic, she supposed, that she, who had always been such a rebel against the rules, now found herself longing for a stricter regimen of rules than she'd ever known. She saw the reasons for them now, in a way she'd never been able to as a kid. She saw the advantages, saw how they kept the community bound together, so that no one, whatever the circumstances, whatever tragedy struck their life, was ever truly alone. She'd seen enough cases of lone survivors where, when all was done and she went back to her office and her life, she was left wondering if they would make it, how anyone could make it when the last connection they had in the world was gone.

In Caleb's world, that never really happened. Whatever the tragedy or loss, there was always the community that pulled together and surrounded the wounded ones. Was that enough to compensate for the crushing of individuality, for the demand for utter conformity?

Right now, she was leaning that way. Perhaps she'd had enough of the ugliness to make her appreciate the positives Caleb's kind of life brought.

As for Caleb himself…

"Hey, lady Amazon, look who's here!"

Sawyer's teasing, unendingly chipper voice

made Emma smile, then sigh. And then Piper was there, chattering excitedly about having someone other than her annoying little brother to talk to over dinner. Which she was just in time for, Piper added, and wasn't she lucky to be here tonight. Margie had gone all out with homemade lasagna—half of which would no doubt be frozen for a rematch later—garlic toast and salad, and as an extra bonus, Julia had made a pan of her delicious brownies for dessert.

She couldn't help smiling at her sister's enthusiasm. The gorgeous girl was going to be a famous TV chef someday, or a supermodel, or, knowing her, maybe both.

She let the chatter wash over her, enjoying it yet not really focused on it. The pain of Caleb's sharp rejection wasn't something to be eased even by the cheerful energy of her younger siblings.

Nor did she have much appetite, even for Margie's delicious meal. Promising to return later for one of the treasured brownies, Emma retreated to the room that had been her refuge throughout her life. If she could not find solace there, then it was not to be found.

Yet instead of what she had half intended, to lie down and rest eyes that were protesting the long hours with a sandy grittiness, she found herself pacing. She tried to focus on the case, but thoughts of Caleb and her feelings for him kept intruding.

Finally, she went to her laptop, booted it up and logged on to her home office system. She called up the images from the Ohio cases and made herself study each young, innocent face. This was why she was here, these girls, and any time she spent musing about her own silly wants was time stolen from them. They'd already had the lives they'd known stolen; wasn't that enough?

...two girls more innocent and pure than any seen in that world.

Caleb's words echoed in her mind. Him again, she thought sourly. But since the words were about the case, she let them stay. And they were true.

She thought about the motives for kidnapping. She discarded the most common, a grab by a noncustodial parent, because that obviously wasn't the case here or in most of the Ohio cases, either.

Ransom. Obviously not likely here, although she guessed the entire Paradise Ridge community would give everything each of them had to get those children back. Problem was, everything they had didn't add up to the kind of numbers usually tossed around in such cases, and there had been no demands made, either here or back in Ohio.

Child stealing triggered by some psychological trauma such as the loss of one's own child usually involved younger children and babies.

And then there was the most telling fact of all, and the probability of it was undeniable. Every victim was an attractive young woman.

And innocent. Pure. As Caleb had said.

They'd known in Ohio this was the likeliest scenario. That the perpetrators had chosen young Amish girls just added a twisted, perverse element to it.

In the world Caleb had spoken so harshly against, innocence was sometimes a very valuable commodity.

A very salable commodity.

She knew Tate was working that end of things, while she continued to dig here. But until they'd found Miriam and Rebecca, she'd dared to hope the girls were too valuable to seriously harm.

Something had changed. And it did not bode well for Hannah or any of the others.

The lights of the huge city spread out below the man lounging in the expensive leather chair. He liked this place and the way it put him above everything. Where he belonged, in his rightful place. It was all in motion: he'd assured his position, made all the right connections; he had all the right people in his pocket, all the way to the hallowed halls of D.C. If President Colton wasn't such a hard-ass, he'd have him in his pocket, too, but he didn't need him. He had everyone else he needed, had a buffer around him that was unassailable.

No one could ever touch him now. And anyone who tried would regret it for as long as they lived. Which might not be long if they refused to get the message.

He smiled, and since he was alone here now, he let every bit of his twisted, warped pleasure show in the expression.

Nothing could get in his way now. He could indulge his every appetite.

And his appetite was growing again. He'd found two at a time, one to enjoy and one to force to watch, was quite stimulating. He'd grown bored with the simpler pleasures, but he thought two at a time might hold him for a while. And after that?

Well, there were always more where those came from.

Chapter 28

"Emma, wake up."

She sat up groggily; she hadn't dozed off until after three, and it was just before seven according to her phone. Her brother was making a habit of waking her up when she hadn't had enough sleep.

"Are you with me?"

Something in his voice, and the absence of his usual teasing greeting, told her she'd better be wide-awake.

"Go," she said.

"I'm sending you something. A video we found online. You'll need to show it to Caleb Troyer."

Her heart slammed in her chest.

"Hannah?"

"I think so."

"Is she…alive?"

"She was."

"How old?"

"Couple of days."

"I'll go right over. He'll be at the shop by now."

There was a pause before her big brother said gently, "You okay, sis?"

"Fine."

"You sure you're not in over your head?"

"I'm an FBI agent, Tate. I—"

"I didn't mean on the job."

The Colton family grapevine was obviously in perfect working order, she thought wryly. And maybe other sources. Tate seemed to have them everywhere. She hadn't thought she'd betrayed her tangled feelings, but Piper in particular had a sharp knack for reading people, and she'd honed it on her family.

"Yeah. Well."

"Just be careful," Tate warned. "And be sure, before you do anything…rash."

Rash, she thought as they disconnected. Yeah, that would be the word for it. And *foolish, impossible* and a few other adjectives.

But calling it every name she could think of didn't change the simple fact; in the short time she'd known him, Caleb Troyer had come to mean more to her than any man she'd ever met.

Don't worry about it, she told herself as she scrambled to get ready. *You're about to blow his life to bits. That should take care of it.*

She watched the video herself as it downloaded. Mindful of the spotty cell service, she saved it rather than trust on being able to stream it at Caleb's. Besides, she wanted to know just how bad it was.

She almost breathed a sigh of relief when she saw it. Yes, it was Hannah, she was almost positive, but she was indeed alive and looked in good shape, except for appearing dazed, probably drugged. It appeared she, along with others, were being paraded for sale, advertised as fresh and "untouched." A marketplace for virgins, for men with sick appetites.

It could have been much, much worse. And Caleb's words about her world shot through her mind again. What kind of world did she live in when something like this video could be a relief?

There was nothing she wanted less than to show this to him. She didn't want to see that look in his eyes, that condemning of the evils she dealt with, condemnation that she couldn't help feeling extended to herself. Yes, Hannah was alive—at least at the time this had been recorded—but who knew where she was or what kind of shape she was in by now. She thought about it all the way as she drove to Caleb's shop, where she guessed he would be by now.

When she got there, the door was unlocked. At least she assumed it was unlocked; maybe he never locked it, although he had a lot of tools in there.

She eased the door open. The main workroom appeared empty. Quietly, she made her way back to the corner that served him as an office.

He was bent over the drafting table. But he was

not working. His elbows were on a drawing that had a slashing mark across it, and his head was resting in his hands, his shoulders slumped. He looked exhausted.

She felt a tightness in her chest, a sort of aching that startled her with its strength. She wanted nothing more in that moment than to be able to ease this man's pain. And instead, she was here to add to it. True, she had proof his sister was alive—or at least had been two days ago—but seeing her like this wasn't going to do much to relieve his mind.

His head came up then, as if he'd somehow sensed her presence. He turned, and for an instant she saw something in his face that made her aching heart leap, something bright, welcoming, something that in another man in another place she would have been certain meant he was very happy to see her.

"I am sorry," he said almost hastily. As if he'd feared he would not have the chance to say the words to her. "I should not have said those things. It is not your fault—"

"Caleb," she began, feeling she had to halt the flow of words even though she was relishing what had made him speak them and the expression on his face that told her he indeed was most happy to see her.

"—and I should not blame you," he finished as if she hadn't spoken. Not rudely, but in the manner of one who had thought long and hard about what he would say if he got the chance. "I am…very glad you came back. I should not have let you leave like that."

I don't ever want to leave.

In the instant the words slammed through her mind, she hated her world more than she ever had. Hated that she couldn't just revel in Caleb's warm welcome, hated that she couldn't seize this moment, couldn't seize him and beg him to figure out a way to make this work between them.

But instead she had to add another harsh layer to his pain. And she couldn't find the words to even begin.

"Emma," he said, his brows furrowing as he

looked at her, as he realized something was wrong.

"I must show you something," she said.

"Hannah?"

"It is…proof she is alive."

For an instant his countenance brightened, but he kept his gaze on her face, and it faded. "You do not look happy about this."

She couldn't answer. Instead, she set her tablet on the drafting table, cued up the video Tate had sent and silently tapped the play arrow.

Emma didn't watch it again. She didn't need to. She remembered with grim vividness the sight of the young women being paraded before the camera in various states of undress. The voice-over, a man with more than a bit of a New York accent, was lurid and lewd, rife with suggestions of what could be done with and to these prime, pure and untouched young girls. For a price.

A very steep price.

She couldn't bear to look at Caleb's face as he watched, caught only the setting of his strong jaw in her peripheral vision.

But she had to make sure.

"This one is Hannah?" she finally asked, pausing the video as the most striking, a slender girl with a long tumble of red hair and wide eyes—drugged, Emma noted with a spurt of anger—and utterly angelic features came to the fore.

"Yes." Caleb said it flatly, and Emma realized he was angry. He had every right, but he was so even-keeled most of the time, it was...

It was a relief, she thought with rueful self-knowledge. It meant he wasn't perfect. It also meant he was capable of powerful emotions, even if he did, either by nature, culture or both, keep them strictly in check most of the time.

"Caleb—"

"How can this be God's will?" he said softly. She knew much more of his culture now, enough to know questioning was frowned upon. Then he looked at her, and his eyes were fierce.

"Men like this...who do this evil...this is who you hunt."

"Yes."

He turned back to the frozen image. Stared for

a moment before saying, in the tone of throwing caution to the wind, "Then as much as I dislike it, I am glad there are such as you to do it. May God forgive me, I want them…"

Punished? Even dead? It's what she would have wanted, in his place. But she'd learned a bit more about the ways of the Amish since she'd been here. She chose her words carefully.

"It's a dilemma, isn't it? Free will and God's will? But who's to say He wouldn't use people to do His will? In this case, to capture and punish those who violate those most basic laws?"

His gaze shifted back to her face. "You…are wise, Emma."

She held her breath. Made herself meet his gaze levelly. Something shifted, changed, grew between them.

"And you are beautiful. And in your heart… good."

"I think," she said, almost hesitantly, "you have your pronouns tangled. All of that applies, yes. But to you."

She thought she saw the faintest trace of color

rise to his cheeks. But he didn't look away. Instead, slowly, he lifted a hand. It seemed to her to take an agonizingly long time, but finally he cupped her cheek. She hadn't realized how much she'd longed for the touch of his work-roughened hand until it was there. She turned her head just enough and pressed her lips to his palm. And had the satisfaction of seeing him shiver, even as a ripple of needy sensation went through her from head to toe.

"What can we do?" she asked, hating the helpless sound of her voice. "Is this impossible? Is there any way?"

"I…" He stopped. He flicked a glance at her tablet, at the image frozen there like a billboard advertising the depravity of her world.

"I know," she whispered, lowering her eyes. "My world…I don't blame you for wanting to stay apart from it. Right now, I wish I could."

"But could you? Could you leave it?"

Her gaze shot back to his face. He meant it rhetorically; that was all, wasn't it? Still, she answered as honestly as she could.

"For the first time in my life, I think I could."

She heard a sound from him, as if his breath had caught in his throat. She knew the feeling.

She made herself restart the video, setting the image of the dazed, beautiful Hannah back in motion. She had apparently been saved for last, as the most striking offering. In the last instant before she was led away, Hannah glanced back toward the camera. She said something or at least tried to.

It looked like *Help me.*

The fear that filled her eyes stabbed at Emma like one of Caleb's wood chisels. It echoed through her, wild, consuming, the memory of that kind of soul-deep fear.

She had lived that once. She had sworn she would spend her life seeing that no one else had to. Obviously, she had failed. Perhaps it was a battle that couldn't be won.

Fury boiled up in her at that thought. Maybe the bigger battle, against perverts like this everywhere, couldn't be won.

But this one could. And she was going to do it.

She was going to bring Caleb's little sister home.

Chapter 29

Caleb wasn't used to being angry.

It wasn't that he didn't feel anger. He was human, so of course he did. But he had been raised to control it, to submit as the church taught. So he had learned, over the years. And it had served him well, especially with the girls. They needed the example he could provide, especially since their ever-patient mother was gone.

But he was angry now. The pure evil before him and the fear in his little sister's eyes were enough to push him swiftly to the edge of even his considerable control.

It was the anger he could see in Emma's eyes

that cooled his own. Her reaction was fierce, almost violent, and in the face of such rage his own began to fade.

"I will never give up," she said, each word driven and sharp like a nail digging into hardwood. "I will find Hannah and I will bring her home."

"And what will be left of you then?"

His own words surprised him. But he could not forget that night she had spent trembling in his arms, reliving her own hideous nightmare. It explained the ferocity of her reaction. She had to be remembering her own feelings of helplessness, the pain and terror she'd endured during her own horrible captivity.

How could she do this? How could she go on? Surely she deserved some peace, after what she had been through? She had fought the good fight for years; surely she had earned some rest?

He realized with a little jolt of self-awareness that, as bad as this gnawing fear and worry about Hannah was, he was nearly as concerned for Emma.

"Your demons drive you," he whispered.

She whirled on him as if the words had been accusation instead of observation. "Shouldn't you be glad of that? It will keep me going until I bring Hannah home."

It was a moment before he could answer, a moment before he admitted to himself he could not stop the words that were going to come.

"I believe that you will. But at what cost? You must face those demons, Emma. You cannot hide them, or hide from them, forever. They will not stay neatly in the box you have built for them."

She didn't speak, just stared at him, pale, her eyes wide, as if she were desperately trying to do just that, push those demons back into their box.

"You must learn how to be peaceful again, Emma. And that must happen from the inside."

As if it were a physical thing, a boiling, churning flow of hot emotion, he saw the anger drain from her. And when she spoke, her voice was so small it broke his heart, coming from this brave, confident woman.

"I don't know how to do that."

"You can learn," Caleb said, taking her by the shoulders, willing her his strength in this moment when her own seemed to be failing her.

She looked up at him, and everything she worked so hard to keep hidden, the haunted woman, the weary battler, the pursuer of too much evil, was there in her face.

"Will you teach me?" she whispered.

His breath caught at what he read in her expression then. For that moment, she let down the mask completely, let him see the vulnerability, the uncertainty, the…love.

The emotion he'd worked so hard to tamp down rose up inside him, blossoming, meeting and embracing what she was letting him see. He could still see fear in her eyes, but he knew instinctively it wasn't haunted memories or the ugliness she fought that caused it; it was simply that she'd been afraid to offer him this.

"I cannot," he said, but regretted the words when she stiffened and started to pull back. He realized she thought he was rejecting her. And as soon as he realized that, he realized that he never could. She had brought him back to life, had shown him his heart still beat, still yearned, had shown him that perhaps he was not finished with love as he had assumed since Annie's death.

"I cannot," he said again, tightening his grip on her shoulders, pulling her close. "No one person can teach such a huge lesson." He smiled at her before adding softly, "But my people can."

He saw her face change as she looked up at him. As if he were somehow a sun that warmed her, the fear left her. He knew in that moment he could not be a coward in the face of her courage.

"And if my love will help you, you have it," he said, his voice rough but steady.

"Caleb." She breathed his name almost prayerfully.

"Is it just me, Emma?"

She looked startled for an instant, then smiled, and he had the feeling she had run the words spoken when she had asked the same through her mind as often as he had.

"No," she answered simply.

And then she smiled, as if for the first time she believed, believed that there was another path for her to walk, a path where not everything reminded her, where she could regain her faith in the goodness of people. He engulfed her in his arms then, aching inside as he held her, as she nestled against him willingly, eagerly.

It was impossible. Emma knew everyone would say it, but they didn't know her, didn't know her strength, her determination and her need for what these people and their way of life—and this man—could offer.

"There must be a way," he said.

"We'll find it," Emma said.

"Your work—"

"There need to be people who do what I do. I just can't be one of them anymore. I will find Hannah, Caleb. I will find her and bring her home. But after that—"

"It will be a very long task. There is much you would have to learn." He said it reluctantly, as if he feared scaring her off but wanted to be fair.

She was under no illusions about the size of the task before her.

"I know. In more ways than one."

"You are certain? This is not a decision to be taken lightly."

"I'm not taking it lightly. But I must get off this path, where every case reminds me and destroys another piece of what little faith I have left in humanity."

She was coming back to herself now. And with every passing moment her certainty grew. She was done. She would finish this case, because it was so crucially important to her, but after that... She nodded once, sharply, confirming her own thoughts.

"I would leave anyway. The battle will continue without me. I've given it enough."

"The girls," he began.

"I adore them. Each in their own way."

"And they already like you a great deal. But it is asking a lot, for someone not used to our ways."

"I can learn. And I would like them to meet my family. Soon."

This seemed to please Caleb immensely, for his smile widened despite his worry over Hannah. She looked at him steadily, letting her suddenly lighter, happier expression take on a touch of mischief.

"I'm not a submissive woman, Caleb Troyer," she said with a bit of her old fierceness.

He laughed. "You think I do not know this?" Then, seriously, he added, "What agreements we reach behind closed doors are our business."

And when she reached up to cup his cheek, when she felt the sudden tension in him, heard the catch in his breath, she began to long for the nights when those agreements would be negotiated.

Hannah would come home.

She would turn from this grim path she walked.

She would have three very different, charming little girls in her life.

And in the simple surroundings that were so

wonderfully steady, unchanging, perhaps she really could find peace.

And with Caleb by her side, she would find so much more.

With an eagerness she'd not felt in a long time, she kissed him, flinging herself headlong into her destiny.

* * * * *

WEB_M&B_RTL3 LP

Discover Pure Reading Pleasure with

MILLS
BOON®

Visit the Mills & Boon website for all the latest in romance

Buy all the latest releases, backlist and eBooks

Find out more about our authors and their books

Join our community and chat to authors and other readers

Free online reads from your favourite authors

Win with our fantastic online competitions

Sign up for our free monthly eNewsletter

Tell us what you think by signing up to our reader panel

Rate and review books with our star system

www.millsandboon.co.uk

 Follow us at twitter.com/millsandboonuk

 Become a fan at facebook.com/romancehq